The Book of
ANSWERS

By A. L. Tait

The Ateban Cipher

The Book of Secrets
The Book of Answers

The Mapmaker Chronicles

Race to the End of the World
Prisoner of the Black Hawk
Breath of the Dragon

The Book of ANSWERS

AN ATEBAN CIPHER NOVEL

A.L. TAIT

Kane Miller

A DIVISION OF EDC PUBLISHING

First American Edition 2019
Kane Miller, A Division of EDC Publishing

Copyright © A.L. Tail, 2017
First published in Australia and New Zealand in 2017 by Hachette Australia
(an imprint of Hachette Australia Pty Limited), this North American
edition is published by arrangement with Hachette Australia Pty Ltd.

For information contact:
Kane Miller, A Division of EDC Publishing
5402 S 122nd E Ave
Tulsa, OK 74146
www.kanemiller.com
www.myubam.com

Library of Congress Control Number: 2018942388

Printed and bound in the United States of America

5 6 7 8 9 10

ISBN: 978-1-61067-828-5

Cover design: Kat Godard, DraDog

For Bronwyn and Christine
Who taught me all about sisters

CHAPTER ONE

Gabe had never imagined it was possible to feel this cold and still be able to move. Surely his hands had frozen on the reins? And his nose, the only bit of his face other than his eyes not covered by his cowl, was numb. Gabe tried to wiggle his toes inside his chunky leather boots, but felt nothing.

"Stop wiggling, Sandals," Gwyn shouted, frowning up at him from under the close-tied hood that covered her white-blond hair. "You're upsetting Bess." Gwyn was leading Bess by the bridle, picking a path through the rocks and stunted shrubs that adorned Hayden's Mont.

The castle in the clouds.

Squinting a little in the dull light, Gabe could just make out the silhouette of the tiny fortress, which seemed to grow directly from the craggy outcrop on which it was built. The keep rose from the heart of a ring of thick, dark walls, perfectly positioned for a view of the entire valley below.

"I'm freezing," Gabe moaned. "Can't I walk with you? At least it might keep me warm."

He couldn't believe how quickly the weather had changed, from the warm sunshine they'd left behind at the foot of this cursed mountain, to the dull, gray clouds and howling wind they'd walked into halfway up. And still they seemed no closer to the castle.

"You're safer where you are," was all she said before turning back to the path, murmuring to Bess, who whickered in response.

A screech above them drew Gabe's eyes upward, and he could see the tiny dot that was Albert, Midge's peregrine falcon. Normally, Gabe loved watching the bird flying in ever-widening circles until he was cruising the sky almost beyond sight. Then would come the incredible dive as Albert swooped on an unsuspecting bird, mid flight . . .

But not today.

Today even the mighty wings of Albert were struggling against the wind.

Gabe shifted in the saddle, trying to find a comfortable seat. After weeks of hard travel, there wasn't a spot on his body that wasn't sore. As he moved, the package tucked into the back of his breeches shifted, digging into him, and he reached behind to adjust it – and to reassure himself it was safe.

The Ateban Cipher. The whole reason that Gabe was here, struggling up a bleak and stony slope with his friends.

When Brother Benedict had implored Gabe with his dying breath to keep the book safe, Gabe had no thought beyond obeying, little able to imagine what that might mean. Even now, weeks later, Gabe didn't know what the book was, or why he had to bring it here, to a cold, barren mountain on the other side of the kingdom from his home at Oldham Abbey.

All Gabe knew was that the men following him were desperate to stop him, and he couldn't let the precious, mysterious book fall into their hands.

Gabe had wrapped the book tightly in its oilskin pouch that morning. Even now, he could see its worn brown cover in his mind, the gilt-edged pages that, when fanned ever so slightly, revealed, as though by magic, an image of the very castle Gabe was now looking at.

It was the only clue that this book of secrets had given up so far.

Twisting in his seat, Gabe turned to check that the others were still trudging up the path behind them. Midge and Eddie were keeping Borlan a safe distance behind Bess, knowing that the stallion preferred to lead. Both of them were sitting on Borlan's back, but tiny Midge was laid along his strong neck, her dark-brown hair blending with the horse's black mane as she whispered in his ear. Eddie rode as though in a parade, straight and tall, his dark hair whipping around his face and his cloak flapping behind him.

Merry was leading Jasper, the third horse, while Scarlett rode, but Gabe knew the cousins were taking it in turns. They were also having the most trouble with their mount. Even now, Gabe could see that Jasper's eyes were rolling and his tail was flicking wildly back and forth as Merry clung to his bridle, her cap of red curls dancing. Scarlett bit her lip, her beautiful face white under the hood of her dark-gray cloak, but she said nothing.

Gabe could understand the horse's fear. He didn't really want to go any farther up this nonexistent path either.

Turning to face forward again, Gabe could see only the sharp, forbidding slopes above them. If they were finding this part of the climb difficult, how were they ever going to manage what lay ahead? He breathed out hard. They would just have to manage. Hadn't they managed to travel the length of the entire kingdom of Alban, staying one step ahead of what seemed like half an army, for more than three weeks?

And now they were so close.

"Do you really think we'll be there by nightfall?" Gabe shouted to Gwyn over the wind.

"I hope so," she said, not turning to look at him. "Ronan will catch us today if we're not."

Gabe gulped. "He's that close?"

"Closer," Gwyn said, still trudging doggedly up the slope. "I've done everything I can to slow them down but . . ."

Gabe shuddered. Gwyn had been backtracking every night, keeping an eye on those who followed them, including the feared Ronan of Feldham, sheriff and chief torturer for Lord Sherborne, and Whitmore, once the head of the King's own guard.

A shout behind him broke through Gabe's reverie, and he twisted in his saddle once again, just as a high-pitched squealing began. To his horror, Gabe could see Jasper rearing up on his back legs, with Scarlett clinging to his mane, trying to keep her seat as Merry clutched for his bridle.

Midge glanced behind her briefly and then concentrated all her efforts on keeping Borlan calm as Eddie jumped down from the saddle and moved quickly to secure the stallion's head. Gabe knew it was the right thing to do – if Borlan reacted to Jasper's fear and ran, all the horses would follow – but it left Merry and Scarlett on their own with a huge problem.

Without thinking, Gabe slid from the saddle and ran down the path towards the rearing horse. "Wait!" Gwyn's voice was sharp on the wind. "Don't!"

But with Gwyn's hands tied managing Bess, the only one who could help Merry and Scarlett was Gabe.

Desperately, he tried to remember everything that he'd learned during his season in the Abbey's stables. Every boy at Oldham Abbey had spent three months in every section of the Abbey to help them to decide on their life's work. For Gabe, the season spent in the stables had been long, slow and, frankly, smelly, and he'd been glad to leave the dark, cool building for his season in the Scriptorium.

Now Gabe wished he'd paid more attention.

All he could remember was the stablemaster's stern voice telling him to stay calm at all times.

Easier said than done.

But there was one other thing . . .

"Merry!" he shouted over the wind and the horse's squealing. "Are you okay?"

"Don't shout!" she said without looking at him, doing her best to avoid Jasper's flashing hooves. "You'll only make it worse."

Gabe slowed, trying to creep close enough so that she could hear him without his having to shout.

"You need to get him to move forward," Gabe said, noting that Merry cocked her ear towards him, though she kept all her attention on the horse. "He can't rear and walk forward at the same time."

She nodded, lifting her eyes to Scarlett, who was still clinging desperately to Jasper's back, holding fistfuls of his mane to keep her balance.

"Scarlett, we need to make him run."

"What?" Scarlett shrieked, and Jasper danced again.

"Forward," Merry continued, trying to sound confident.

"I'll get the others out of the way," said Gabe, turning to make his way back up to Borlan.

"Move him off the path," Gabe said to Eddie, who nodded, eyes on Midge. The small girl agreed and between them they began the slow and gentle process of convincing Borlan to move sideways, while Gabe dashed farther up the path to give the same instructions to Gwyn.

"Makes sense," she agreed, tugging gently on Jasper's bridle. "I only hope that Scarlett can hold him once we clear the way."

Gabe gulped. He hadn't thought of that. To get Jasper to move forward, Scarlett would need to give him his head – and once he had that, who knew how far he might bolt?

"She'll be okay," Gwyn went on and Gabe thought his face must have given away his fear. "Scarlett's been on a horse since she was two years old, even if she did have to learn to ride sidesaddle to keep her father happy. The only one who's better in the saddle is *him* . . ."

She pointed to Eddie before turning back to Gabe, gray eyes alight with mischief. "Not that I'd ever let on to Scarlett that I thought he was better."

Gabe couldn't hold back his grin as he imagined that particular conversation, but it was wiped quickly from his face by the sound of thundering hooves and shouting behind him.

Gabe looked up just in time to jump out of the way, catching sight of Scarlett's grim face and flying braid as Jasper flashed past him close enough to throw rocks up into Gabe's face. Feeling as though he'd swallowed a stone,

Gabe watched in horror as the horse rushed headlong up the rugged slope, heedless of the peril that every step held for him – and for Scarlett.

"That's it," breathed Gwyn beside him, her own eyes glued to the unfolding scene. "That's it, bring him in nice and slow."

And, as Gabe watched, that's exactly what Scarlett did, not trying to bring the horse up hard – which would probably result in her being thrown over his head – but allowing him to run even as she tightened her grip and shortened the reins, easing Jasper into a canter and then a trot and then, at last, a walk.

By the time they came to a halt, Jasper had raced half a mile farther up the hill and the only sound that Gabe could hear was his own heartbeat pounding in his ears, louder even than the howling wind.

"Well," breathed Merry, coming to stand beside him to watch Scarlett slide from Jasper's back and grab his bridle. "We probably didn't need that right now."

Gwyn peered around Bess's great head. "No," she agreed. "But it will happen again. We need to protect the horses. They'll have to go back."

Gabe stared at her. "Go back?"

"Yes," Merry said. "Gwyn's right. We'll need to take them back down the mountain and keep them safe."

She stopped, squinting up at Scarlett still standing quietly with Jasper, seemingly not willing to make a move.

"I'll go with Midge and Scarlett," Merry said. "We'll hide in the woods while you, Gabe and Eddie sort out this book business and then we'll head for home as soon as we can. Winterfest is not far away now."

Gwyn's jaw set in a hard line at her sister's words, and she nodded. Gwyn had only one reason for being on this mountain, Gabe knew, and it had nothing to do with him or the Ateban Cipher. No, Gwyn was here because she and Merry had decided that taking him to Hayden's Mont was the best way to save their pa, Ralf Hodges, from being hanged at Winterfest, a mere three weeks away.

"I'll take Sandals and the Prince," Gwyn was saying now. "Don't get too comfy down there in the autumn sunshine – we'll be back before you know it."

Merry laughed. "Given that we've got to get three scared horses around Ronan and company, who are probably struggling up these very slopes as we speak, I'm not thinking there'll be too much lounging about."

"Oh yes," said Gwyn, thoughtfully. "Ronan. See if you can slow him down, will you?"

"Don't worry," said Merry, with a wink. "I'm looking forward to that bit."

Gabe shook his head at their tone as the rising wind blasted his face. "How can you joke about this?" he asked, rising fear making his tone sharp. "Scarlett nearly got killed and the rest of us are probably not far off."

Merry threw an arm around his shoulders, her cloak flapping behind her. "Don't fret, Sandals," she said. "Pa always said that fretting just makes everything harder. The best thing you can do right now is to focus on getting up that hill. Midge, Scarlett and I will deal with what's behind us."

Gabe swallowed, trying to calm the swarm of bees that seemed to have taken up residence in his stomach. "Sorry," he muttered, realizing that she was right. Worrying about what might happen or what had nearly happened wasn't going to help them now.

"Would it help you to say a little prayer or something?" Gwyn asked, looking earnest but uncomfortable.

"What?" asked Merry, looking as surprised by the suggestion as Gabe was. "Are you going to hold hands and pray with him?"

"No," said Gwyn, and Gabe was touched by how uncertain she seemed. "But we all have our rituals and Sandals here has been without his for weeks now. I need him calm to get him over the final hurdle so, you know, whatever works . . ."

Her words trailed away uneasily as Merry and Gabe continued to stare at her.

"Thank you," Gabe said, reaching out to touch Gwyn on the arm. "I'm okay now."

Gabe wasn't sure why, but he didn't want to share with the girls the fact that he still prayed every day, in the morning when he woke, and at night when he went to bed. The wonderful thing about prayer was that it didn't need to be said out loud to reach its destination and he found that it helped him to make sense of each day.

He hadn't realized before he'd left Oldham Abbey how important the rituals of daily life within its walls were to him. Like every other novice and oblate, Gabe had grumbled about having to go to the chapterhouse six times a day, never understanding for a moment how much he'd miss it if he ever had to leave.

Mostly because Gabe had never imagined leaving.

"Well, if everyone's okay now, you'd best get going," Merry said, still looking at her sister with a strange expression. "The sooner you leave, the sooner you're back."

"And the sooner we're back, the sooner we can save Pa," said Gwyn, any sign of that brief hint of uncertainty gone. "Come on, Sandals, let's deliver that book."

Gwyn reached into the pack she'd tied to Bess's saddle, unearthing the small bag that Gabe knew contained half-a-dozen boiled eggs and a few handfuls of berries – the last of their food supplies.

"We'll take these," Gwyn said to Merry. "You'll be able to forage once you're back in the woods, but there's not much to eat up here."

Merry nodded, before taking hold of Bess's bridle and leading her back onto the path, facing down the slope.

With her free hand, Merry dragged her sister to her for a short, fierce hug.

"Take care," Merry said.

"Always," Gwyn answered.

Then Merry was gone, leading Bess towards Midge, Eddie and Borlan. Moments later, Eddie was striding up the hill, his ratty brown cloak flying behind him. "We're to tell Scarlett to follow them down," he said.

Gwyn nodded, before turning to lead the trio up the rocky slope. "Stay close, boys," she said over her shoulder. "If you thought it was hard on horseback, you're in for a real treat."

Feeling the stones slipping away under his feet as he picked his way up the path behind her, Gabe looked up at the gray, barren hillside that awaited them.

High above them, a small black dot against the leaden clouds, Albert screeched, the shrieking echo bouncing off the rocks around them.

❖

"Surely no castle in the history of castles has ever been so well placed to hold off an attack," Eddie panted, pulling himself up onto the narrow ledge beside Gabe. "How in the world do they get their supplies up here?"

Gabe didn't have an answer for that even if he'd had enough breath to speak. It had been only two or three hours since they'd left the horses, but the hard uphill trudge made it feel much longer. Rain spattered on his cloak, and Gabe pulled it closer around his body, trying to keep out both moisture and chill.

"Back door," said Gwyn, quietly, sitting on the ledge on Gabe's other side. "Just like the tunnel at Rothwell, only we don't have time to find it so we just have to knock at the front."

"If we ever get there," muttered Eddie.

"Oh, we'll get there," said Gwyn. "Well, I will."

Her grim tone left the boys in no doubt that she'd go without them if she had to.

"You can't leave us here," said Eddie. "You need me to get you in the door, and Gabe's book is the whole point of the exercise."

Gabe looked from one to the other, taking in the cold steel of Gwyn's gray eyes and the haughty self-confidence in Eddie's. It was Eddie who had brought them to Hayden's Mont, right up on the border between Alban and Caledon. He'd recognized the fore-edge painting as being the same as one that his father, the King, kept close to him in his solar at the royal palace.

But now Eddie was as much a fugitive as Gabe, and an imposter pranced around Rothwell Castle in his place. An imposter placed there by Lord Sherborne and his henchmen Whitmore and Ronan.

"I'll find a way to get in the door," Gwyn said, after a moment. "And I don't need Sandals to take the book."

Eddie snorted. "But you do need me to present myself before Lord Lucien," he said, haughtily. "It will be hard to get a letter proving I'm the rightful Prince – and therefore able to win a King's pardon for your father – without *me*."

Lucien was a former Brother who had stormed from the royal palace after an argument with Eddie's father many years earlier – and never returned. Eddie was pinning all his hopes on Lucien to prove his real identity.

Gwyn fixed him with a hard look. "The only reason I am here with you is that Merry asked me," she said. "Given the choice, I would have spent the last month back in Rothwell discovering exactly which dungeon they spirited my pa into and getting him out of it. But Merry knew you had *no chance* of winning back your crown without us – and so here we are."

Eddie's silence was the only response and Gabe hid a tiny grin under his hood. He didn't really think that Gwyn would leave them behind, but that didn't mean he didn't enjoy watching her put Eddie in his place every once in a while.

Nobody else could do it quite the way Gwyn could.

"Can we move?" Eddie asked.

"Yes," said Gwyn, allowing Eddie to change the subject. "It's time. That rain is only going to get harder and I for one don't want to spend the night here with you two."

Gabe got to his feet, groaning. He was covered in bruises from slipping and sliding his way up the slope and his legs were aching from walking on an angle for hours. Lifting his face up to the light rain, he tried desperately to summon up strength from somewhere within him.

"I could really use a roast dinner – pheasant, potatoes, fresh minted peas, thick, rich gravy," Eddie said, making Gabe salivate at the thought. "Those boiled eggs were a long time ago."

Gwyn's peals of laughter echoed off the stone walls around them. "Well, keep dreaming," she said, edging her way along the ledge, back to the wall, until she disappeared around a rocky outcrop. "Whatever it takes to get you to the castle doors."

Ignoring his growling stomach, Gabe followed, keeping a sharp eye on the crumbling edge of the ledge, trying to keep his feet, which were substantially larger than Gwyn's, on solid ground. Glancing sideways, he noted that Eddie was even worse off. The soft leather boots he'd been wearing when Lord Sherborne's henchmen had kidnapped him were now worn and full of holes, and uncomfortably close to the abyss.

"Look down there," Eddie said, and Gabe leaned forward slightly to peer over the edge. Down below, he spotted a group of dark figures struggling up the slope. Squinting, he picked out Ronan of Feldham bringing up the rear, wearing the bright-red cloak that signified his allegiance to Lord Sherborne. The man was waving his arms around, trying to drive his long-suffering soldiers up the mountain, his hard face a menacing mask.

At the head of the group, however, was an even more frightening figure – tall, dark and dressed in black.

Whitmore, the man who had been the Prince's personal guard. The man who had betrayed him, allowing Lord Sherborne to throw Eddie into a dungeon and put an imposter in his place.

"I see my loyal servant continues to have my best interests at heart," said Eddie, with a wry smile.

"He does seem to want to catch up with us," Gabe said, trying to match Eddie's tone.

"Yes," said Eddie. "And to bring along nine others to keep us safe."

Gabe managed a chuckle. "At least they had to leave their horses behind as well," he said.

"Indeed," said Eddie. "We'd all have been better off riding mountain goats up here."

"Come on, you two." Gabe looked up to see that Gwyn had somehow managed to climb up onto a huge boulder above them and was standing, hands on hips, looking down. "I don't think the view's that good that we need to hang about."

"No," said Eddie, dragging his eyes away from the group below. "No, I've seen better."

"Well, quick sticks then," said Gwyn. "Get yourself up here. I've a mind to play skittles."

Puzzled, Gabe cautiously made his way around the ledge and followed Gwyn's path up the cliff face. He reached Gwyn's side, Eddie panting behind him, to find her wedged against the rock face, her feet tucked in behind the boulder on which she'd been standing.

"Ready?" she asked, eyes alight. "Hold my arm, Sandals – just in case."

Gabe took hold of her arm. "In case of wha–?" Gabe's words were cut off as Gwyn suddenly thrust hard with her feet against the boulder, dislodging it and sending it crashing down the mountain. Pulled off balance by the shift in her weight, Gabe clutched at her with his other hand, managing to grab hold just as Gwyn's feet went out from under her and she slid towards the edge of the ledge.

Feeling his own feet sliding on the path, Gabe desperately tried to hang on to her, throwing his weight back – relieved when Eddie grabbed him around the waist. Slowly but surely, Eddie walked backward, bringing them all back to solid ground.

"What were you thinking?" Gabe asked, fear making him angry. "You could have killed yourself – and me!"

Gwyn merely grinned. "And yet, here we are, thanks to our very own heroic prince," she said. "And look!"

Both boys looked over the ledge, following the huge rock's bouncing path as it hurtled down the mountain in the rain – directly at the dark figures below. As they watched, the group split, diving in all directions as the rock passed over them, looking for all the world like ninepins.

Gwyn brushed her hands together before wiping dirt and water on her cloak. "That should slow them down for a moment," she said. "They'll be worried there'll be another one."

And with that, she was on the move again, dashing along the wet, narrow ledge as though running through the forest.

"Come on," Gwyn urged, not stopping to look behind her. "It will be dark soon and we need to be behind those doors before the moon rises."

As he hurried after her, Gabe realized he didn't want to spend a night on one of these narrow ledges and the idea of three feet of solid stone and thick wooden doors between them and Ronan of Feldham was attractive, to say the least.

But it was hard to ignore the small voice in his mind that wondered if Lucien would even let them in.

CHAPTER TWO

"I don't think anyone's home," said Eddie, his relaxed words undone by the anxious squeak in his voice.

"Oh, they're here all right," said Gwyn, once again hammering on the door. "Look at the knocker."

Gabe walked over to inspect the huge ring in her hand. "It's just a knocker," he said.

"It's a *polished* knocker," Gwyn corrected. "Look at the shine on it."

"Putting aside the fact that you would even bother to *have* a knocker all the way up here," Eddie began, "why does it matter that it's polished?

Gabe and Gwyn exchanged looks. "Because it's recent," said Gabe, before Gwyn could jump in and highlight Eddie's lack of knowledge of common household tasks. "Given the rain up here, which feels as though it might be permanent, it would have dulled if it had been done more than a day or two ago."

Eddie nodded, frowning.

"Plus," said Gwyn, drawing out the word, "there's the fact that if you look through the keyhole, you can see a faint glow." She grinned impishly.

Gabe laughed faintly, bending to take a look. "There's a fire lit in the hall," he said. "And here I was thinking you were a soothsayer."

Gwyn went back to hammering on the knocker and Gabe wandered over to stand beside Eddie, who was peering about him in the gloom.

"It's a funny place, isn't it?" Eddie said, and Gabe could only agree. The closer they'd gotten to Hayden's Mont, the more it became apparent that the reason it was portrayed as tiny in the painting on the book wasn't just because of its lofty position, but because it *was* tiny.

Usually a castle consisted of walls with guard towers, a large inner courtyard, and a keep, inside which you'd find the residence of whoever owned the place. But this building had its own design, clearly defined by its location. The outer ring of thick stone walls was set against a towering rock wall, which disappeared ever upward to form the peak of the mountain.

The entrance to the castle was approached by a set of stone stairs that drove through the walls at the center, splitting the ring in two and ending at two huge wooden doors. The stone walls stretched up on either side of the staircase, merging seamlessly into the looming stretch of stone that formed the front wall of the keep.

Looking behind him now, back down the stairs, Gabe noticed the strong portcullis set into the entrance arch, not far from the step. He shivered, realizing that if the heavy iron trellis was suddenly lowered, they'd be trapped here, in a stone prison, between the portcullis and the castle's front doors.

"I'm thinking they don't really like visitors," said Eddie, also looking at the portcullis.

"You wouldn't live here if you liked visitors," Gwyn said, coming over to join them. Gabe didn't miss the note of admiration in her voice.

"Look," she continued, without a breath, "I'm going to go and open the door – it's at least dry inside, even if our welcome is not warm. You two wait for me here."

"How are you going to open the door?" Eddie asked, and Gabe could almost hear his teeth grinding together.

Gabe caught the flash of Gwyn's smile in the dark. "Don't worry," she said and was gone, back up the steps towards the door.

"I am *not* going to just stand here," Eddie muttered. "Follow me."

Gabe trailed up the steps after him, feeling the oilskin pouch for the 500th time to check the book was still safe. The string was still slung around his body, under his cloak, and he'd become so used to the weight of the book in the small of his back that he hardly noticed it now.

By the time the two boys reached the top step, there was no sign of Gwyn. The stone walls loomed around them, dark, forbidding sentinels, while the timber doors seemed to stretch upward forever, disappearing into yet more stone.

"Where is she?" Eddie hissed. Even in the gloom, Gabe could see that the generous top step was bare, with nothing in the corners. A slight noise overhead drew his attention upward.

"Up there," Gabe pointed.

By the light of a rising moon that seemed to flicker behind heavy, scudding clouds, they could make out a small figure flat against the dark-gray wall, arms and legs outstretched as it crawled, spiderlike, up the stones.

As Gabe watched, mouth dry, Gwyn paused to brace against a vicious gust of wind that threatened to lift her sideways from her precarious perch. As it subsided, she reached up once again, appearing to feel around with her hand, then, satisfied she had a handhold, she bent her knee, jamming her toes into a tiny crevice between the stones, and lifted her body up.

A noise at the bottom of the stairs dragged Gabe's eyes from Gwyn's painstakingly slow progress. Peering down, Gabe saw nothing but a wizened twig, blown up from who knew where by the swirling wind, but he was suddenly very aware of just how exposed the three of them were. The stone walls created a canyon, which was perfect for defense as any would-be attacker was trapped at the bottom while those inside could no doubt rain rocks and hot oil down from the tooth-shaped battlements above.

But it also meant that if Ronan of Feldham appeared at the bottom of the steps any time soon, then Gabe and Eddie were sitting ducks. Gwyn, Gabe and Eddie had managed to dislodge several more rocks on the way to the castle, but who knew how long it had delayed the men.

Gabe assumed that Ronan wasn't the type to stop when he was so close to his prey, no matter how dangerous the going might be in the ever-deepening dark.

"Eddie," Gabe said, tugging on his friend's cloak to grab his attention. "We need to get the portcullis down."

Eddie turned to him. "And how do you propose we do that?" he asked. "The winding mechanism will be operated from inside the walls."

"I don't know," Gabe admitted. "But if Ronan and Whitmore arrive before Gwyn gets the door open, we're both going to be caught."

Eddie's glance swept upward, to where Gwyn clung, halfway up the walls, before nodding, his jaw tight. As quickly as they could, the two boys made their way down the steps in the gloomy light.

Standing under the archway that housed the portcullis, Gabe could feel his hopes sliding away. He could see the wicked points that marked the bottom of the trellis, but they were a long way up from where he stood – and there seemed no way to bring them crashing down to close the gate.

"You check that side and I'll look over here," said Eddie, heading to the right-hand wall. "There must be *something*, surely. No castle builder would ever rely on just one defense."

Feeling as though he was wasting his time, Gabe's eyes scanned the left-hand side of the archway, noting the way that each trapezoidal block wedged perfectly into the next, all the way up to the keystone, the central stone that held the arch in position. Admiring the craftsmanship, Gabe reached out to touch one of the weathered stones, and as he did so, he remembered the dungeons below Lord Sherborne's castle – and the secret door hidden in the stone wall, which had allowed them all to escape from the dungeons with Eddie.

Wishing he had more light by which to see, Gabe used his hands to examine the archway, noting that the walls here were broader than both his arms spread wide. Getting down on his hands and knees on the rough cobbles, Gabe ran his fingers across every brick, desperately searching for any hint of a deep crevice that he might use to pry open the door.

"Anything?" Eddie asked.

"Nothing," said Gabe, sitting back and looking up at the underside of the arch, which seemed to taunt him with its perfect smoothness. He pulled his cloak around him, wishing the wind would disappear and take with it the whistling around his ears.

"Me neither," said Eddie, coming over to slump beside him. "Well, there's a pattern carved into the cornerstone, but that's it."

"A pattern?" repeated Gabe.

"It just looks and feels like the plan for the archway," said Eddie, but Gabe was already on his feet, making his way to the cornerstone.

Peering at the dark-gray stone, he could see that Eddie was right. It looked exactly like a builder's drawing for the archway, showing the pattern of trapezoidal stones, with the keystone in the middle. Feeling it, however, Gabe discovered that the trapezoidal shapes were carved *into* the rock, but the keystone had been carved *out*, so that it stood out in relief against the stone.

Frowning, Gabe pressed his fingers against the keystone shape, but nothing happened. He tried to place his fingers on either side and turn the shape. Nothing.

Frustrated, Gabe stood up and kicked hard at the keystone, glancing up to see how Gwyn was progressing up the stone wall. To his surprise, she was almost to the top, within reach of the battlements.

As he turned to let Eddie know, his mouth dropped open. His friend was disappearing into the yawning darkness of a small doorway that had opened up beside him.

"You did it!" said Eddie, sticking his head back out of the doorway. "There's a staircase in here that must lead up to the battlements."

Shaking his head as he dashed under the archway to join Eddie, Gabe realized that the keystone shape he'd kicked must have been an ingenious trigger stone for the door. Pulling the section of wall closed behind him, Gabe found himself in total blackness.

"Eddie?" he called out softly.

"Up here," came Eddie's voice. "Once you're on the bottom stair there's only one way to go. Use the walls to feel your way up, and watch the steps – they're uneven."

Following the sound of Eddie's voice, Gabe kept one hand on each side of the narrow walls, despite the damp slime under his fingertips. The steps, he realized, were just as slippery, winding around in a clockwise direction, every one set to a different height. Any attacker who made it this far would be surprised and at a terrible disadvantage, Gabe thought.

At last he reached the top of the stairs, which widened into a round room featuring a row of six arrow-slit windows across the side that Gabe, thoroughly disoriented from his winding walk in the dark, assumed was the front of the castle, overlooking the valley.

"Look!" said Eddie, his voice muffled by the fact that he had his face to one of the slits. "You can see the whole mountain and valley from here!"

Gabe crossed the room quickly, looked out the slit next to Eddie, and gasped. The view down the mountain and across the valley had been dramatic enough from the front door. Up here in what was obviously a turret below the battlements, it gave him an idea of what the world must look like to Albert.

"Eddie," he said, grabbing his friend by the arm. "Can you see down there?"

Below them, struggling up the rocky slope towards the castle gates, was a dark, shadowy mass that Gabe supposed was Ronan of Feldham, Whitmore and their soldiers, huddled together for warmth against the icy blasting wind.

"Whitmore!" said Eddie. "Gadzooks! I didn't think they'd be foolish enough to continue that ascent in the dark."

"There's no time to lose," said Gabe, dashing from the tiny window and feeling his way around the walls until he came to the chain that secured the portcullis. "We need to hold them off as long as possible."

To Gabe's surprise, it was the work of just minutes to unwind the chain from its hook on the wall and send the portcullis crashing down to lock the staircase below. If Eddie also noticed that the well-oiled chain was at odds with the uninhabited feel of the castle entrance, he said nothing.

"Right," said Eddie, striding back towards the stairs. "Let's go."

Moving as quickly as he dared down the irregular staircase, Gabe could hear Eddie panting ahead of him, his feet tramping a staccato beat on the stone stairs. At the bottom, they paused, and Gabe listened to the faint sound of shouting and a creaking, rattling noise, suggesting that Ronan and company had made it to the gate and were trying to shake the portcullis to raise attention.

"Come on," said Gabe, "open the door." As much as he hated the idea of stepping onto the main entrance stairs in front of Ronan of Feldham, Gabe wanted to get to the front door before Gwyn opened it.

"I can't," gasped Eddie. "I can't find a handle or anything to open it. I can't even find the door. It's like it's disappeared."

Gabe's heart sank as he realized that the door must fit as seamlessly into the wall on this side as it did on the other. Meaning there was another secret trigger stone somewhere in the dark, narrow space in which they stood.

"We have to find another keystone," he said, frantically feeling along the walls, wishing he could see his hand in front of his face. "Gwyn's inside the castle by herself and we must get to her before she opens the door. She'll be worried that something's happened to us if we're not there."

A few minutes later, though, Eddie sighed. "It's no use," he said. "We'll never find it in the dark. We've got to find another way out."

"What do you mean?" Gabe asked, still running his hands over the stones, looking for a crevice, a depression, a bump, anything . . .

"This room has to have another exit," Eddie reasoned. "Otherwise anyone who gets trapped up there in an invasion is stuck for good. I think that turret is under the battlements. We need to go up and into the castle to find Gwyn."

Without a word, Gabe followed his friend up the stairs. If there was any chance Eddie was right – and given Gwyn's words about the back door to the castle and the secret door into this turret, it seemed that whoever had built this castle had thought of every possibility – then it was better to chance their luck inside the castle than to waste time searching for the trigger stone.

"It won't be in the walls this time," said Eddie, standing in the center of the room, squinting upward. "We need a light!"

"Well, we don't have one," reasoned Gabe, whose many years in the Abbey had taught him to make do with what he had. "So what else can we do?"

He reached above his head and discovered that if he stood on tiptoe, his fingertips grazed the low timber ceiling. Eddie, who was that bit taller, would be able to place his own palms flat.

"We're going to have to feel our way around and see if we can find . . . something," Gabe said. "You start on the side away from the stairs, I'll begin here."

Working in silence, the boys made their way around the circular space, but found nothing.

"Take one step into the center and go again," said Gabe. "We'll need to cover every inch to make sure we don't miss anything."

It was on their seventh revolution that Eddie called out, "Got it!"

In the darkness, Gabe could hear him grunting, and then a rasping sound followed by a sudden blast of cold wind.

"A trapdoor!" said Gabe, moving to stand beside his friend, welcoming the freshness of the night air even as he felt his face start to hurt under its icy embrace.

"It must take us right to the top of the parapet," said Eddie, jumping up to grasp the edges of the open space and pulling himself up through the hole. "Come on, let's get going. Lord only knows where Gwyn is by now . . . If we can stop her opening the front door, all the better."

As Gabe reached up, allowing Eddie to drag him up through the open space, he imagined Gwyn's surprise when she opened the front doors – as he had no doubt that she would – to discover the staircase empty and a group of angry soldiers rattling the portcullis.

Gabe grinned to himself in the darkness as he landed in a heap on the stones above and realized that he was, indeed, at the very top of the castle battlements. As he pulled his cloak up to protect his ears and face from the buffeting wind, Gabe had the sudden sobering thought that she might not be pleased with their efforts.

Gwyn might go where she liked, when she liked, but she generally liked other people to be where she expected them to be . . .

❖

Inside, the castle was almost as dark as it had been out on the battlements. The boys had hurried along the walk until they'd come to a solid door set deep into walls, the huge main doors of the castle below them.

It was a matter of moments before they were inside, and found themselves on yet another winding stone staircase. This one, however, had the promise of faint light at the bottom, and the boys had gone towards it with relief.

That relief was short-lived, however, when they'd tumbled out at the bottom to find themselves in a huge, empty room, lit only by one tiny fire at the other end.

"This is the Great Hall," whispered Eddie. "At least we're on the right side of the doors now."

Looking at the huge timber doors looming above them, Gabe shivered. They might be on the right side of the doors, but their welcome was anything but hearty.

"Where's Gwyn?" he whispered back. "She should be here."

Eddie looked at him, shadows from the low fire dancing on his face. "You place a lot of faith in her ability to do what she says she'll do," he said.

Gabe lowered his eyes. "She hasn't let us down yet."

Eddie frowned. "She's just a person, Gabe, like you, like me," he said. "Sooner or later people always let you down."

Gabe didn't miss the tinge of bitterness in his voice. "I think Gwyn is different," he said, quietly.

"I didn't think Whitmore was like that either," said Eddie. "Or my father for that matter."

Gabe stopped. "You think your father is to blame for what's happened to you?"

"I –" Eddie began, before stopping, one hand pushing his hair from his eye. "No," he continued, sounding sad. "Not really. But I wish he'd trusted me enough to talk honestly about his health and to . . . help me. If he dies suddenly, I'm left to pick up the pieces. And that Grand Melee we witnessed at Lord Sherborne's palace will be nothing compared to the pushing and shoving that will go on as the court jockeys for power." There was another short silence. "Not that I need to worry about that now," Eddie continued, voice grim. "It's the imposter who will be left to manage."

"Or be managed," said Gabe, remembering the docile, placid features of the boy he'd seen dressed as the Prince.

Gabe had been sure that he'd been drugged, and he feared for the boy's safety.

Once Lord Sherborne and Whitmore had control of the throne, the imposter would no longer be important. He could simply disappear into a dungeon – or worse – and never be seen again.

"Or be managed," Eddie echoed, nodding in agreement. "For all we know it's happening now, while we run around in the dark freezing our noses off."

Gabe took a deep breath and began moving towards the door at the other end of the hall. "All the more reason for us to get moving then," he said. "Lucien must be here somewhere and hopefully he has the answers we need."

"He'd better," Eddie said. "Otherwise, we might as well all hole up here for the rest of our lives – and, frankly, it's too cold for me to want to stay long."

With a longing glance at the smoldering fire adjacent to the carved wooden door, Gabe used his frozen fingers to turn the huge brass handle, wincing at the pain the movement caused.

"I'm so cold I hurt all over," he murmured to Eddie as he poked his head through the doorway, looking left and right down a corridor that appeared endless. There was no one in sight, but Gabe's heart was cheered a little by the sight of the burning sconces that adorned the walls beside every doorway set into the wall – and there were many doors.

"Someone's definitely home," he said to Eddie, over his shoulder, as he stepped into the hall. "These sconces are not long lit."

"Great," said Eddie. "Let's hope they're pleased to see us now that we've let ourselves in."

But, even as the words left his mouth, Gabe heard a huge crashing sound from the left, followed by a deep voice yelling – and a much higher voice shrieking with rage.

"That's got to be Gwyn," said Gabe, already running towards the noise.

"Yes, and it sounds as though she's found a new friend," quipped Eddie, on his heels.

Gabe didn't bother to answer, instead following the noise past doorway after doorway until he arrived at one that showed a crack of light under the door. Without even thinking, he turned the handle and pushed hard, barreling his way into the room.

Gabe had only a moment to take in the fact that he'd arrived in a long room with huge glass windows at one end. Silhouetted against the windows, backlit by candles, he saw the shadow of a woman bent over a spinning wheel, which turned ceaselessly. She did not so much as turn her head towards the door.

Gabe took a step forward, realizing that his feet were suddenly making no sound, due to the thick, warm rugs that lay across every inch of the stone floor, and the walls were lined with enormous and beautiful tapestries in golds and reds, blues and an unusual shade of bright green. A roaring fire spat and leapt in the majestic stone fireplace that took up a quarter of the right-hand wall. Floor-to-ceiling timber bookshelves, crammed with manuscripts of all shapes and sizes, ran the entire length of the left-hand wall.

And, in the center of it, stood a massive man, dressed in a long, dark robe, trying to keep his grip on the arm of a girl struggling wildly at his feet.

CHAPTER THREE

"**G**wyn!" shouted Gabe, taking another step forward before Eddie grabbed hold of his elbow.

"Stop," hissed Eddie. "Stay back. Look at the size of him. He'll only grab you too."

But the man had stilled at the sight of the boys, mouth dropping open, and Gwyn took advantage of his shock. With one final wrench, she freed herself from the huge man's grasp, pelting across the room to stand beside the boys.

"I told you," Gwyn gasped, and Gabe realized she was speaking to her erstwhile captor. "I told you I'm not a thief. Here they are, just like I said."

But the man said nothing, continuing to stare at the boys, eyes flicking back and forth between the two.

"Er, good evening, Sir," said Eddie smoothly, stepping forward with a small courteous bow, despite the water splashing from his still-damp cloak onto the thick rug. "We knocked but . . ." His words trailed away. "Anyway," Eddie continued, raising his head. "I am –"

"I know who you are," rumbled the man, his gruff voice hoarse with age and, Gabe thought, disuse.

Eddie took a step back. "You do?" he asked, surprised.

"You are the image of your father as a boy," the man replied, and his gravelly voice wavered. "Edward. Crown Prince Edward."

There was, Gabe noted, no hesitation in his response. He wondered if the man would be so certain if faced with the imposter, or with Eddie *and* the imposter in the same room. The similarity between the fake Prince and Eddie was, after all, eerily uncanny.

"Then you are –" Eddie began.

"Lucien," the man responded. "Who was once Brother Lucien."

Gabe's eyes widened at the "was once." He'd never met a former Brother before, though Brother Malachy, who had come to the Abbey late, had mentioned in passing several old friends of his who had left the order. Malachy had always thought it was funny that his friends had left the sanctuary of holy life for the wider world, just as Malachy himself was going the other way.

"Lord Lucien," Eddie was saying. "My father has spoken of you."

"Pah!" said Lucien, spitting into the cheerful fire that burned beneath the huge mantel. "Don't speak to me of your father."

Eddie's face went red at the slight. "My father is a good man," he said, voice raised though he maintained his courtly posture and manners.

Lucien's face softened beneath his beetling gray brows, though his eyes remained fierce. "Even good men make bad decisions," he said quietly.

"Well, that certainly clears up one of our questions then," Gwyn interjected, before Eddie could ask the questions that Gabe could see clouding his face. "You're happy to vouch that this is Crown Prince Edward then, are you? Heir to the realm? Lord of all he surveys?"

Lucien stepped closer, peering down at Gwyn from his great height, no sign of stooping in his broad back. Gabe took in his long, gray hair and the wrinkles that lined his forehead and cheeks, and wondered how old he really was.

"Can I assume from your disrespectful tone that you are not?" he asked Gwyn, who simply held his gaze as he loomed over her.

"Let's just say that I've had questions," she said, and smiled.

Lucien stared down at her for a moment longer, before suddenly throwing back his head and laughing out loud. "I think I like you, girl," he said.

"Well," Gwyn answered, with a grin, "I guess that's a step up from where we began."

Lucien laughed again. "Indeed. As to your question . . ." He turned to Eddie. "I don't quite understand why your identity is at issue."

"It's a long story," Eddie began.

"Let us have the short version then," Lucien said, cutting him off.

Gabe listened anxiously as Eddie outlined his situation, explaining that he'd been kidnapped on his way to Rothwell Castle, thrown into a dungeon with Gwyn's father, Ralf, and, once rescued by Gabe and the girls – mostly, the girls, Gabe acknowledged – had discovered a boy in his place on the throne.

As Eddie spoke of his betrayal by Whitmore, captain of Eddie's own guard, his voice cracked, and he swallowed hard.

Lucien listened in silence. "I would ask why you simply did not go home to your father and explain the situation," he said, "but I have seen the King make bad decisions before – perhaps you simply felt that he would not listen?"

"No!" Eddie exploded in anguish. "It's not that at all. My father has been ill these long months. He is as weak as a kitten and can barely lift his head from the pillow. The few times I was able to visit him, he rambled on about the past and I wondered if he even knew that I was there."

He paused. "Whitmore advised I give my father time and space to get better, not to bother him, but now I see . . ."

As Eddie's voice trailed away, Gabe's thoughts raced.

Eddie had told Gabe that his father was ill, but this suggested a man who was close to death.

When Gwyn and Merry had convinced Eddie to go with the group to Hayden's Mont, it was because they believed that if Eddie was to turn up at the castle gate in rags talking about being the real Prince – when the Prince (or the imposter pretending to be him) was known to be safe with Whitmore at Rothwell Castle – he would be thrown into a dungeon before he ever got a chance for the King to recognize him.

But if the King was so weak and addled, perhaps he would never again recognize his own son?

Gabe shivered.

"I see," was all Lucien said in response to Eddie's tale, before turning those strange black eyes to Gabe. "And you? Who are you?"

Gabe looked down at his feet. "I'm Gabe," he said. "Brother Benedict sent me."

Lucien took a step back. "Benedict," he said, and now his voice sounded even more strangled. "From Oldham Abbey?"

"That's right," said Gabe, his confidence growing a little as he realized that Lucien was familiar with Brother Benedict. It was the first real confirmation that Gabe had had that he'd brought the precious manuscript to the right place after all.

But Lucien wasn't at all what he'd been expecting a friend of Brother Benedict's to be – and his reaction to Gabe's words only underpinned that.

"I –" he spluttered, backing away from Gabe.

"Brother Lucien?" said Gabe, taking a step forward. "Are you all right? Do you need a drink of water?" He put one hand under the man's elbow to steady him.

"I'll get it," said Gwyn, dashing across to the fireplace, where six or so mismatched but richly upholstered chairs were arranged in a semicircle with a small highly polished dark timber table to one side. She was pouring water from a crystal carafe into a sparkling glass by the time Gabe had guided Lucien to the nearest chair.

Dropping into it gratefully, Lucien accepted the glass from Gwyn, taking a long sip as Gabe and Gwyn watched anxiously while Eddie hovered behind them. "Are you all right?" Gabe repeated, once again wondering about the age of this man. From a distance he looked strong and capable, and he'd certainly had a good grip on Gwyn. But as he sipped the water slowly, the color returning to his face, Gabe realized that Lucien must be at least near the same age as Brother Benedict had been. Which was to say, ancient.

"Just a shock," said Lucien, his hooded eyes roaming across their faces. "It's not every day I find a thief, a prince and a . . ."

He focused on Gabe briefly before continuing. "You . . . in my library. We don't get many visitors up here."

"I'm not surprised," said Gwyn. "You're not exactly rolling out the welcome mat."

Before Lucien could respond, Eddie slapped his hand on Gabe's shoulder. "Visitors!" he exclaimed. "We need to warn them!"

"Warn us?" said Lucien, his eyebrows drawn together. "Warn us of what?"

"Well, warn you, and Gwyn," Eddie said. "Ronan of Feldham is at the gate."

Lucien frowned. "Feldham? Sheriff of Rothwell? Why would he be here?"

As Eddie filled Lucien in on the broad brushstrokes of their story, Gabe filed away the fact that Lucien knew who Ronan was, which meant that he had a working knowledge of a shire on the other side of the kingdom from his own home. Glancing at Gwyn, Gabe knew that she hadn't missed the significance of that either.

Someone had been keeping Lucien apprised of events far from his home. The question was who? And why?

"Well, now I know why he's here," Lucien said, as Eddie wound down. "But he will keep. This castle has kept out savage hoards, ferocious armies and fly-by-night chancers, so I've no doubt that it's a match for a small band of half-frozen, half-wit soldiers."

Gwyn smirked. "But not us," she said.

"No, not you," Lucien agreed, shaking his head. "And we shall come to how you got in, but first I want to know *why* you're here."

It was as though the room held its breath – even the crackle of the fire seemed to pause. Gabe, feeling the heavy weight of the book pressing into his back, knew that he should simply pull it out and hand it over, but something held him back.

"Go on," hissed Gwyn, elbowing him in the side. "We haven't come all this way for you to get cold feet now, and we really don't have all night."

Given that he was only just now getting full feeling back into his frozen feet, Gabe smiled at her words. But still he hesitated, knowing that once he gave the book to Lucien, he might never hold it again.

"What is it?" hissed Gwyn again, this time grabbing Gabe by the arm and dragging him out of his chair and over towards the door where they couldn't be overheard. "Surely you don't distrust him, not now we've come all this way on the say-so of your blessed Brother Benedict."

It was the mention of the old monk, Gabe's mentor at Oldham Abbey, that jolted him, allowing him to recognize his feelings for what they were: possession, ownership. Having never owned a single thing in his whole life, he'd taken ownership of the book. A book that was definitely not his. A book that Brother Benedict had directed him to bring here.

"Sorry," he said to Gwyn, knowing he couldn't fully explain his actions – and knowing that she would never fully understand his feelings. "I'll give it to him now."

Reaching up under his tunic, Gabe carefully pulled the pouch from his waistband before realizing that he was going to need to undress to unsling it from its position over one shoulder, under his shirt.

"Um, can you turn your back?" he asked Gwyn, who rolled her eyes but did as she was directed, turning on one heel and stomping back to where Eddie and Lucien were now sitting in silence. As Gabe untied his cloak, dropping it to the floor, and reached to pull his tunic up and over his head, he saw Eddie raise questioning eyebrows at Gwyn, who nodded in return.

With the strap of the pouch unslung, Gabe quickly dressed and walked over to Lucien.

"Brother Benedict asked me to bring this to Hayden's Mont," he said, still holding the pouch. "Before I give it to you, though, who else lives here at Hayden's Mont?"

Eddie and Gwyn both looked startled at the question, and Gabe realized that it hadn't occurred to them that Lucien might not be the person that Brother Benedict had intended the book be given to. But Gabe wasn't taking any chances.

"There is just me, two trusted servants and . . ." Lucien's voice trailed away, before he cleared his throat and resumed. "And her. You can understand why we do not open the door to strangers at sundown."

But Gabe was looking at the silent figure still spinning at the other end of the room. She had shown no interest in their conversations and seemed not to have even noticed that three strangers had invaded her home.

"Who is she?" Eddie asked.

"That doesn't matter at this time," said Lucien. "She hears only her own thoughts."

Gabe wondered at the deep sadness on the man's face, but Lucien was holding out his hand for the pouch.

Gabe gave it one last pat before handing it over and stepping back, his mouth suddenly dry as Lucien opened the mouth of the pouch before drawing out the book.

Feeling hot and cold, Gabe could only watch as Lucien drew one reverent finger over the book's worn leather cover.

"The Ateban Cipher," Lucien breathed. "I had heard . . . I never thought . . ."

He placed the book carefully on his lap before fixing his eyes on Gabe. "Benedict gave you this," he said, no question in his voice.

"Yes," Gabe nodded.

"Then Benedict is –"

"Dead, I think," Gabe answered.

"You think?" Lucien looked surprised.

"He was badly injured when I last saw him," said Gabe. "When I went back to check on him with the head of our Infirmarium, he was . . . gone."

Lucien exhaled sharply. "Gone?" he breathed.

"Disappeared," Gabe clarified. "No sign he'd ever been there."

Lucien grimaced, pausing to think before speaking. "But he told you to bring the book to me?"

"Well," said Gabe, "he told me to bring it to Hayden's Mont and then Eddie told me that you were here. As you're the only, er, former Brother here, I guess it's for you."

Lucien said nothing, merely stroking the cover of the book as he stared into space. A thick silence, broken only by the occasional squeak from the spinning wheel and the very faint sounds of shouting that suggested that Ronan had not given up at the portcullis, filled the room as Gabe, Eddie and Gwyn waited for Lucien to speak.

Finally, Gabe could wait no longer. "Well," he said. "What is it? I know the book is called the Ateban Cipher, but what is it? Why do Prior Dismas and Lord Sherborne want this book so badly? Why did Brother Benedict insist I bring it here? *What does it say?*"

He could hear his voice rising with the frustration of weeks of arduous travel, of being pursued for the book, of looking at it every night by the fire, puzzling over its coded words and its beautiful, detailed, other-worldly illustrations.

He hadn't realized until this moment just how much the *secrets* of this book were driving him crazy.

Lucien turned his wrinkled face to Gabe, shaking his head. "I wish I knew," he said, taking the last of Gabe's stream of questions first.

"What?" Gabe almost shrieked, half laughing. "You mean we've dragged that manuscript across the entire kingdom with soldiers at our heels for nothing?"

Lucien smiled. "Well, not for nothing," he said. "You did as Brother Benedict asked you to do. And I can answer some of your questions – just not the last one."

Gwyn shifted in her chair. "Well," she said, quietly but firmly, "could you get on with it then? I can still hear those men at the gate, even if you can't, and I'd quite like to sort this book out, get a letter from you endorsing Eddie as the Crown Prince and be on our way."

Lucien sighed. "I wish it were that simple," he said. "The truth is that this book . . . I cannot keep it here."

"What?" Gabe shouted. "But Brother Benedict –"

Lucien placed one calming hand on Gabe's shoulder. "Brother Benedict would be proud of what you've achieved so far," he said. "But . . ." He broke off, once again picking up the book. "The Ateban Cipher," he said, and Gabe could hear the hint of wonder in his voice. "I never thought that I would see it, hold it. I had heard that it existed. Brother Benedict did his job well. He has kept it safe." He paused. "To understand, I must tell you the whole story," he began.

"About time," Gwyn breathed so that only Gabe could hear.

"The Ateban Cipher," Lucien continued, "is also known as the Book of Answers." He stopped again.

"Answers to what?" Eddie asked.

Lucien sighed. "Everything," he said. "Or so legend has it. No one has ever been able to read the book, though many, from kings to scholars, have tried to unlock its secrets."

"When you say 'everything'?" Gwyn prompted.

Lucien stared at her. "Everything. The meaning of life. How to turn lead to gold. How to stay young forever. How to read the future. Any question you might have, the answer is in here."

Gabe frowned. "But if all of this was once known, why don't we still know it? Why just one book?"

Lucien sighed. "This is an ancient manuscript," he said. "Whoever created it knew the power that such secrets hold. So it was written in code and then somewhere, somehow, the key to that code was lost."

"Leaving no way to read the book with all the answers," finished Eddie.

"Exactly," said Lucien. "But the inherent power of the book remains – the *possibility* that one could know these things – which is why Lord Sherborne wants it, I would say." He paused. "Imagine being the keeper of such secrets – able to make as much gold as you want, to live forever as a young man, to hold the power of life and death over everyone else, to choose the path into the future."

Gabe gulped. "That's why he's working with Prior Dismas," he said.

Lucien stood, still holding the book, looming over Gabe. "Yes," he responded. "It will take a team of scholars to break the code and where better to find the best than an Abbey, particularly one with a reputation like Oldham Abbey's."

"But how did Brother Benedict come to have the book?" Gabe asked, unable to imagine how the modest old man fitted in to all this.

"The keeper of the book is a secret," said Lucien. "To the point where most people, common folk, nobles, Brothers and scholars alike, believe the book to be a myth. Brother Benedict and I were close when we were younger, but we drifted apart when I went to live in the palace as part of the old King's council and he . . ."

Lucien paused, rubbing one hand across his eyes without letting go of the book with his other. "He gave up his role as a talented scribe to take up a position in the Librarium at Oldham Abbey. I couldn't understand it at the time – he was on his way to being one of the finest illuminators ever. But looking back, that must have been when he was given responsibility for the book."

"And now he's given it to you," Gabe said. "Look at the side, the painting."

Lucien sighed, slipping back the cover to take in the beautiful image. "Benedict did this," he said, stroking the fine brushwork. "His work is quite distinct. But I cannot keep the book." He slipped the cover back and held the book out to Gabe.

"Too many people know where it is," he said, waving the book. "Not just you three, but those who clamor at the gates."

"They don't know I have it for certain," said Gabe, glancing at the others, refusing to take the book. "They just think –"

Lucien waved the book again to cut him off. "The fact that they even think it is enough," he said, pacing back and forth. "They will not rest until they turn this castle upside down and find it. No," Lucien said. "You must take it with you. I'll hold them off as long as I can to help you get away."

Once again, he held the book out to Gabe. "What?" said Gabe, unable to believe his ears, feeling as though he was about to cry. "You want me to take it away again? But where?"

"I'm sorry, Gabe," Lucien said, his grizzled old face sad. "I really am. I know it's been a difficult journey, but we must keep the book safe at all cost."

"Where will we take it?" Gabe asked, finally taking the book from Lucien's hand as he realized the older man was deadly serious. "I don't know what to do with it."

"Why don't we just throw it in the fire?" Gwyn asked, jumping to her feet, voice shrill with impatience. "If it's this much trouble and nobody wants it because everyone wants it, let's just destroy it and get back to the others."

"NO!" said Gabe and Lucien at the same time.

"Why not?" said Gwyn, hands on hips, gazing defiantly at both of them. "No one can read it anyway."

Eddie nodded. "She's right," he said. "Why not just solve the problem by destroying it?"

Lucien shook his head. "Because we can perhaps *help* people if we can unlock the secrets," he said. "We don't actually know what's in the book – only the rumors and whispers that have passed down the years."

Gabe nodded his agreement. "Plus," he said, "it's the most beautiful thing that any of us have ever seen. For that reason alone we can't destroy it."

Gwyn studied him, head cocked to one side. "Okay, Sandals," she said, ignoring Lucien. "So if we're not going to throw it in the fire, what are we going to do with it?"

Gabe frowned. "I guess if Brother Lucien can't be the keeper of the book, then we have to find someone else to do it," he said, before looking up at Lucien. "Right?"

Lucien smiled. "Oh, I don't think you'll have to look far for that."

"What do you mean?" asked Gabe.

Gwyn dug him in the ribs again with her sharp elbow. "You, Sandals," she said. "He means you. You're the new keeper of the book."

"That's right," said Lucien, glancing over at the shadowy figure near the windows. "And now you must leave."

"But –" Gabe began, as Lucien started ushering them towards the door, suddenly impatient to be rid of them.

"Not without my letter," said Eddie, stonily, ignoring Lucien's attempts to move him. "My father – and, perhaps more importantly now, his advisors – will listen to you, even if I turn up looking like a street urchin. And I can't get the imposter off the throne without it."

"And not without some food," said Gwyn, rubbing her stomach, also standing her ground. "I'm starving."

"All right," said Lucien, and Gabe wondered why he was suddenly so flustered. "Follow me to the kitchen and I'll write your letter while you pack some supplies."

"It's pitch-black out there!" Eddie complained. "Surely we're safe enough in here for the night?"

"Lucien?" The old man stopped in his tracks at the sound of the low, musical voice. "Is something the matter? Who are these children?"

"My lady," Lucien began, as they all turned to face the woman who had left the spinning wheel and moved, as silently as a specter, behind them. "It's nothing, go back to your spinning."

But the woman just stood there, one white hand over her mouth, staring blankly at the group. It took Gabe a moment to realize that she was staring directly at him.

"Dylan," she gasped, reaching out one white arm towards Gabe, who shrank back from her grasp. She was the palest human being he'd ever seen, from her lank white hair to the ethereal, floating white gown she wore.

"My dear," Lucien began again, but the woman was not listening to him. Instead, she tiptoed, trancelike, towards Gabe.

"Dylan," she whispered. "Is it really you?"

Gabe shook his head, backing away from the haunting need in her face. "I'm not Dylan," he said.

"No one else has those eyes," she cooed, clutching at his arm. "Green as grass, deep and wide. I knew you'd come for me."

Gabe tried to snatch his arm from her fingers, but she was stronger than she looked. "I'm *not* Dylan," he tried again.

"Aurora," Lucien interjected, striding over to remove her hand from Gabe's arm. "You are scaring our guest."

"Oh," she said, looking confused. "But –"

"Aurora?" Eddie said, at the same time. "Aunt Aurora?"

Eddie was looking back and forth between the woman, who seemed to have disappeared into her own dazed thoughts, and Lucien, his own confusion apparent.

Lucien sighed. "I hoped it would not come to this," he said.

Eddie put his hands on his hips, suddenly looking every inch the Prince. "But this *is* my Aunt Aurora?" he questioned. "The one my father told me died before I could remember her?" He stopped suddenly, his face white. "She's the reason you fought," he said, slowly. "This is why you left the palace and never came back." Eddie paused, staring at the woman who was now looking off into space, as though she was alone in the room. "She's the reason there's a painting of Hayden's Mont in my father's solar," he said, no doubt in his voice.

Lucien looked pained. "Yes," he said, nodding.

"But –" Eddie paused again, this time looking at Gabe, and back at the woman. "Who's Dylan? And why does she think that Gabe is him?"

"I –"

"The truth," Eddie demanded, drawing himself up. "Now."

"Very well then," said Lucien, head bowed. He took a breath before continuing, and Gabe noticed that Eddie did the same, as though he recognized that they were about to hear the story of why Lucien had stormed from the royal palace so many years before, after arguing with Eddie's father, the King.

"Dylan was a troubadour," Lucien began. "He was a singer, a poet, a musician, and the love of your aunt's life."

Eddie gasped, but Gwyn put a hand on his arm.

"And?" she prompted.

"And," Lucien said, as though the words were being pulled from his throat, "the father of her baby."

Gabe frowned. "But what does that have to do with me?" he asked.

It was Gwyn who answered. "I would say," she said, turning to face him, "that you are the spitting image of your father. Am I right?"

She turned back to Lucien, who nodded, looking exhausted. "Yes," he said. "Gabe, there's no easy way to say this . . ."

Gabe swallowed, feeling as though the room was spinning. "She's . . ."

"Yes, Gabe," said Lucien, his voice sounding very far away. "Aurora is your mother."

CHAPTER FOUR

Gabe opened his eyes slowly, taking in the silent circle of faces leaning over him: Eddie, Lucien, Gwyn.

"Gabe?" Gwyn asked, softly, and it was her use of his first name, rather than the taunting "Sandals," which brought it all flooding back.

His mother. In this room. But not, Gabe realized, looking down at him with loving concern.

He sat up, wincing as the room swam and the back of his head began to throb. "Whoa," said Eddie. "Don't move. You hit your head when you –"

"Fainted," Gwyn finished.

But Gabe ignored them, his eyes pinned on the woman who was, even now, drifting back towards her spinning wheel, humming to herself.

"She's not . . . herself," said Lucien, seeming to read Gabe's thoughts. "She hasn't been herself since the King banished her from the palace after driving Dylan to his death."

Eddie stiffened. "My father would never kill a man," he said. "Not outside of war."

Lucien shook his head, sadly. "There are more ways to kill a man than running him through with a sword or hanging him by the neck," he said. "Dylan was not a hard man. He loved his music and he loved Aurora. When the King took both of those things from him, and locked him up, he simply faded away."

Gabe licked his lips. "He died in prison?"

Lucien nodded.

"And . . . my mother?" Gabe watched the woman, once again a dark shadow at the spinning wheel.

"She, too, is locked way," said Lucien, "albeit inside a world of her own making when reality became too much for her to handle. That's why you ended up at the Abbey. She was in no fit state to care for a bairn so I . . ."

"Took me to your old friend Brother Benedict," Gabe finished, wincing.

Lucien nodded. "It seemed the best solution at the time."

As he stared at the figure bent over the spinning wheel, Gabe's mind whirled with memories of his life at the Abbey, where he'd always been content and safe. The woman at the spinning wheel was a stranger to him and there was no logical reason he should be feeling the incredible sense of loss that surged within him when he looked at her now.

"Gabe?" Gwyn's voice broke his reverie, and he turned to her. "I know this is difficult," she began, before hesitating.

The understatement almost made him smile and Gwyn seemed encouraged.

"The thing is," she continued, sounding much more like her normal self, "we have to go."

Gabe was instantly alert. "Can you hear something?" he asked, cocking his head to listen for the sounds of the soldiers shouting at the gate.

She shook her head. "That's just it," she said. "I can't. We have to go."

Gabe knew that Gwyn's instincts were uncanny. He glanced once again at the woman near the window – he couldn't even think of her as his mother – and then down at the book in his hand.

"You're the keeper of the book," Gwyn reminded him. "You need to keep it safe."

Gabe said nothing, stroking the book's cover, as Aurora began to sing softly to herself, oblivious to the tension in the room and the danger at the gate.

"I know this is hard," Gwyn tried again. "If anyone knows, I do. But you have to look after the book. We can't let it fall into Lord Sherborne's hands. Neither the book, nor Eddie. It's your duty."

Taking a deep, shaky breath, Gabe nodded. Gwyn did know how he felt. Hadn't she left her father behind in

Lord Sherborne's dungeon to keep Eddie safe? True, she hadn't known who Eddie was at the time, but she'd done what her father asked her to do. She'd done her duty.

"Right," said Gabe, tucking the book back into its pouch and slinging it over his shoulder. Not allowing himself a backward glance at the woman near the window, he strode towards the door.

"Er, which way are we going?" he asked, as he reached for the handle.

"Kitchen first," said Lucien, "then I'll show you out."

Gabe paused. "I'm assuming we're not going out the front door?"

Lucien chuckled, though the sound was humorless. "Not this time," he said.

❖

"I wish there was some way to let Merry and the others know we're on our way," said Gwyn, through a mouthful of cheese and bread. "They won't be expecting us in the dark and it will ruin any lead we might have on Ronan."

"Well, unless you want to run down there and tell her, we'll just have to take our chances," said Eddie, gnawing on an apple, watching as Lucien wrote the letter that identified Eddie as the rightful Prince.

Lucien had led them, through a warren of hallways, down into a surprisingly cheerful and well-stocked kitchen before setting his words to parchment. Now, he carefully notarized the letter with a wax seal, using the large gold ring he wore on his left hand to make the mark.

Once the wax signature seal was dry, Lucien folded the document into thirds and sealed it once again. "I want to make sure there's no question," he said, handing the letter to Eddie, who looked at the double seal with interest. "Your father will know that I always seal important missives twice."

While he'd been writing, the others had set about hanging their sodden cloaks before the roaring fire. They'd then started filling three small canvas bags with as much food as they could carry – and there was a lot to choose from.

"Where did you get all this stuff?" asked Gwyn, hanging off the larder doors in amazement. The wide, deep shelves of the cool space were packed full of sacks of grain and sealed preserving vessels.

"Oh, we are well served by the local community," Lucien said, focusing on his document, while Gwyn and Gabe looked at each other, eyebrows raised.

"What community?" Gwyn asked. "We passed no town or village on our way to the foot of the mountain."

Lucien smiled at her. "They're not at the foot of the mountain," he said. "You'll see."

Gwyn let the larder doors close with a slam, before turning to lean against them, looking deep in thought.

"Do they just deliver regularly?" she asked, as Gabe shook his head at her persistence. Why did she care so much about how Lucien and Aurora ate?

"No," said Lucien, also looking perplexed. "We ring the bells," he explained.

"Bells?" said Gabe, finally catching up with Gwyn's thought process. "We can use them to alert Merry!"

Gwyn considered a moment, before she reluctantly shook her head. "It won't work," she sighed. "It will probably just alarm the girls and they'll think something's happened to us."

"No!" said Gabe, feeling his excitement rising, happy to have something to focus on that didn't involve the strange woman upstairs. "I know a way that she'll know it's just for her."

Eddie stared as Gwyn frowned. "How are you going to do that?" he asked.

But Gabe simply turned to Lucien. "How many bells in the peal?" he asked.

Lucien looked bemused. "Fourteen," he said. "In the key of C major."

"Great," said Gabe, relieved. "We only need four."

⌖

"Right," said Gabe, looking around the circle of faces. "Everyone ready?"

Eddie and Gwyn nodded, each holding the thick rope in front of them.

"Don't move until I signal you," Gabe said. "Gwyn, whistle the tune."

Gwyn pursed her lips and whistled the short melody that she and Merry had learned from their father. The tune that Gabe had heard in the forest the first night he'd met the girls, when he'd been wandering around in the dark, certain he was being set upon by thieves.

"Again," he said, concentrating hard, hands around two separate ropes. "And then again."

She began again and he let her get to the end before nodding to Eddie.

"You," Gabe said, and Eddie pulled hard on his bell, reeling the rope so that it pooled at his feet. The ear-numbing deep bong of the bell reverberated through the tower, almost knocking Gabe off his feet with its power. These bells must be even bigger than those at Oldham Abbey, ensuring the sound would be heard for miles around.

The rope was barely snaking back up again before Gabe nodded at Gwyn and then, almost in the same breath, pulled hard with his right hand, adding the rings of two higher bells to the tune. Gwyn was nearly lifted from her feet by the thick rope and she jumped as it dragged her up, enjoying the ride.

Gabe had no time to even smile at her glee, as he let go of the rope he'd pulled and put both hands on to the left-hand rope, adding the highest of all the bell sounds to the chorus.

"Now," he shouted to Eddie, who gave his rope another huge pull and the big bass bell sounded once again.

"Let go," Gabe yelled, and the other two dropped their ropes, listening to the clanging above them as it echoed away. As the last note sounded, Gabe once again picked up his ropes. "Twice more," he said. "So they realize it wasn't just an accident."

"Do you really think they'll recognize the tune in the bell peal?" Eddie asked, preparing himself for another round.

"Scarlett will," Gabe said. "You heard her sing in the tunnel under the dungeon. Perfect pitch. She'll hear it."

He nodded to Eddie, who pulled the rope hard, and they began the five-note tune again.

As the bells jangled joyfully above them, Gabe could only hope that Scarlett, Merry and Midge would read the message that Gwyn was trying to send them.

He had the feeling they were going to need every advantage they could get in the race back to Rothwell – a feeling that wasn't helped by the sudden appearance of Lucien's head through the trapdoor at the top of the bell tower ladder, worry written all over his face.

"Are you done?" he shouted over the clanging of the bells.

Gabe nodded, letting go of his ropes as the others did the same.

"Good," said Lucien. "There's no time to waste. Ronan of Feldham has breached the walls and he and his men are searching the castle. The ringing bells will only give them somewhere to aim for." His head disappeared.

Even as Lucien was speaking, the bells were dying away.

"Pull them again," Gabe ordered. "Any order. Make a noise!"

The other two did as they were told and the resulting cacophony nearly deafened them. "Harder!" shrieked Gabe. "Right," he said after a moment. "Now run!"

They slithered down the ladder as fast as they could while the bells rang out above their heads. Lucien waved to them from the doorway before disappearing again, his robe swishing through the opening after him.

"What was that last bit about?" asked Eddie, as they dashed after the older man. "All that noise!"

"It will keep the bells ringing longer," explained Gabe, hurrying to keep up with Gwyn who had scampered ahead of the two boys. "If you get enough swing in them they just keep going."

"Ah," said Eddie, looking at him sideways, eyes alight. "Ronan will think we're still there!"

"That's the idea," said Gabe.

After that, there was no more chat as they raced along the stone halls as fast as they could. Lucien moved remarkably quickly for a man who Gabe thought must be well into his seventies, but then, it was perhaps not surprising given the solid, almost youthful strength of his upright form.

As they ran, Gabe calculated that they were heading away from the gates towards the back of the castle, which nestled into the brooding bulk of the mountain behind it. It seemed strange to be running away from the gates and the walls, and deeper into a building inhabited by Ronan and his men, but Gabe was more concerned about something else.

"Will she be okay?" he panted to Lucien as they half ran, half slid down a narrow, winding staircase, hoping that wherever they were going was nearby. For some reason, it was much harder to breathe up here on the mountaintop. Gabe felt as though he was having to drag hard for every gasp of air.

"If you mean Aurora, then yes," said Lucien, glancing down at him. "I gave her the signal to hide before we went to the bell tower. She won't be found."

Gabe nodded, still struggling to come to terms with the idea of the vacant-eyed woman as his mother, but glad nonetheless that she had not been left alone and defenseless. He pushed away the questions clamoring in his mind. He had no time to think about anything other than the Ateban Cipher now. He was the keeper of the book and it was his job to keep the precious manuscript safe. With Ronan of Feldham and Whitmore searching the dim halls of the castle, that was more than enough for him to think about.

Gabe reached behind for a reassuring check that the book was still in place. He had become so used to the weight of the pouch tucked into his waistband in the small of his back, that he had to physically touch it with his hand to be sure it was there.

"Still there, Sandals?" came Gwyn's teasing question. "Where do you think it will go?"

Gabe forced a laugh. "I'm taking no chances," he said.

To his surprise, she didn't come back at him with a mocking rejoinder. "Good," Gwyn said instead. "Maybe you're finally learning something."

"Shhh," said Lucien, and Gabe realized that the older man had stopped dead just a few feet in front of them, having reached the opening of a narrow corridor that ran off the main hallway. "Quietly now. I can hear them."

Gabe could also hear the faint sound of voices, which seemed to come from somewhere overhead. The thick stone walls and floors of the castle muffled all but the loudest noises, but it sounded as though Ronan and Whitmore had been to the bell tower and discovered their ruse.

"We have only minutes before they're upon us," said Lucien. "It's time to split up. You go that way and I'll go back to meet them. I'll hold them off as long as I can."

Eddie, Gwyn and Gabe looked at each other. "Go that way, where?" asked Eddie.

Lucien's teeth flashed white in the dim light. "You'll see," he said. He turned to Gabe. "Look for the wolf, which hides the door, and keep the book safe. Tell them I sent you."

He turned to leave, his robe flapping behind him as he moved back the way they'd just come.

"Wait!" Gabe called out, and Lucien turned. "If you meet Whitmore and the others, won't they know that you don't have the book?"

Lucien smiled. "Not if I don't tell them," he said. "This is a big castle. I could have hidden that book anywhere."

Gabe gasped. "They'll torture you," he said, thinking of all he'd heard about Ronan of Feldham, of the cold menace he'd seen in Whitmore's face the first time Gabe had laid eyes on him outside Oldham Abbey. "They'll kill you if they think you're hiding it from them."

Lucien's face was impassive. "All the more reason they should not get their hands on that book," he said. "Imagine a world in which people like that have the Ateban Cipher."

Lucien turned to Eddie. "Bear witness," he said. "Go straight to your father. Tell him what you've seen. Tell him you know about Aurora. Tell him . . ." He broke away, staring at the floor for a moment before once again looking at Eddie. "Tell him I made a mistake too, and that I have missed my dear friend these past long years."

Lucien returned his attention to Gabe, looming over him. "Now go," he said, his voice suddenly gentle. "But don't forget to come back. I think that you have your own questions, which can only be answered here."

With that he was gone, leaving Gabe and Eddie to stare at each other.

"Are you coming?" hissed Gwyn's voice from the other end of the narrow hall. "I've found the wolf."

She was kneeling on the floor at the very end of the corridor. Reaching her side, Gabe saw that she was pressing her fingers into the indentations around one of the stone tiles on the floor. Leaning in, he could see the faint outline of a tiny wolf carved into the stone.

"A wolf," said Eddie. "The symbol of my family. This castle must have been an outpost for us since ancient times."

"Still is, if you ask me," said Gwyn, still pressing at the tile. "Probably no better place in the world to keep your aunt safe, and it would have been the perfect place for the book . . ."

"If we hadn't brought Ronan of Feldham and Whitmore right to the door," said Gabe, sadly, hating the fact that their arrival had dispelled the peace and safety of his mother's life.

"We'll have all the time in the world to discuss this once we find this door," said Gwyn, standing up in frustration. "I can't figure out how to open it."

"Let me have a try," said Eddie, muscling his way forward.

Gwyn stood back with an ostentatious mock bow. "Be my guest, Your Highness," she said, her gray eyes alight with mischief, despite the pressing danger.

"We don't have time for you two to start a fight," Gabe reminded them, startled by a loud thump overhead. "We have to go! It will be the same as the other door, Eddie – kick and stamp until you find the trigger stone."

"I'm trying, Gabe," Eddie ground out, and Gabe could hear weeks and weeks of hard travel, frustration and anger rising up. The travel north hadn't been easy for a boy used to the finer things in life, though, to his credit, Eddie rarely complained. Not that anyone would have listened if he had.

But the harsh sound of boots on stone was suddenly closer, and Gabe had no time to feel sorry for the other boy. "They're coming," he hissed, casting an anxious glance over his shoulder. With any luck, anyone passing by would overlook the narrow opening to the hall, but he didn't want to have to rely on that.

"You keep trying," Gwyn ordered Eddie. "Sandals, with me."

Gabe crept back along the hall on his tiptoes, wincing at the sound of Eddie stamping the stones behind him, and hoping that it only sounded so loud because he was so anxious. Holding his breath, he watched as Gwyn flattened herself against the right-hand wall and stuck her head through the opening, quickly glancing left and right, before hurriedly withdrawing and stepping back to whisper close to Gabe's ear.

"They're at the bottom of the stairs," she said. "Whitmore and two others."

"What do we do?" Gabe gulped.

"We go and help Eddie," she said, disappearing back down the hallway.

Gabe was about to follow, when the sound of heavy footsteps halted. "You – that way," Whitmore growled, and one set of boots began walking . . . away from the corridor.

Gabe heard Eddie curse under his breath, the wolf stone clearly not giving up its secrets, and his heart sank. Surely time was running out . . .

"They're here somewhere," Whitmore bellowed. "There's no way past the guard at the front gate, and no other way out."

Gabe felt a tiny surge of relief at his words – Lucien had so far managed to avoid his "visitors."

"That old fool is not talking yet," Whitmore went on, dashing Gabe's hopes, "but that book is somewhere in this castle and those kids are the key to finding it. They can't hide from us forever."

Gabe began tiptoeing back towards Eddie, knowing that they *had* to get out of this corridor right now. There was nowhere to hide and if Whitmore got his hands on Gabe, he got his hands on the book.

"Any luck?" he whispered, as the soldier with Whitmore rumbled a deferential response to his words and Gabe heard the sudden, worrying tread of heavy boots making their way towards them.

"Nothing!" said Eddie, though Gwyn simply kept kicking at different stones. "I –"

His words died away as the wall behind him suddenly slid open, revealing a deep, black, yawning hole.

"That's it!" said Gwyn, keeping her voice low and pointing with her toe to the anonymous stone that had proven to be the keystone. "Now let's go before that big oaf discovers there's a back door." Without hesitating, she stepped through the door, disappearing into the darkness.

"Come on," came her disembodied voice. "Get in here so that we can work out how to close the door behind us."

Glancing once again over his shoulder, towards the sound of advancing footsteps, Gabe did as he was instructed, stepping out of the dim corridor and into the complete blackness that awaited him beyond the door.

❖

Gabe knew which way was up and which was down – but that was about all he knew. The darkness around him was thick and airless, the spiraling ramp beneath his feet endless, and the wall beneath his hand rough and comforting, the only solid thing in a world that felt increasingly out of balance.

"You still with us, Sandals?" Gwyn asked from her position at the head of the line. With her uncanny ability to find the right direction and, probably, to see in the dark like a cat, she sounded perfectly at home.

"I am," he said, giving the string that held them together a little tug. Even as Eddie was sliding the door to the staircase closed behind them using the lever located just inside the door, Gwyn had insisted that Gabe pull the string from the oilskin pouch holding the book and put it in her hand.

"Hold that end," she'd said to Gabe as he'd tucked the book back into his waistband. He'd done as instructed, grasping the end of the string, and then she'd told Eddie to grab the middle. It was only a relatively short piece of string, so they were walking close together, but, as Gwyn had said to them, at least they wouldn't lose each other in the dark.

Gabe had the strange sensation that he was not moving at all, but rather was suspended in the blackness. He had a sudden memory of his hours trapped in the anchorite's cell beneath the altar at Oldham Abbey. Then, he had

had to lie down on the floor to get his bearings. He could only imagine Gwyn's mocking laughter if he tried that now, and so he fought against the sudden longing to feel the earth close to him.

Darkness really could be suffocating.

"Where do you think we're going?" Eddie's voice came suddenly out of the black, and the hint of squeak in it told Gabe that the Prince's nerves were also wound tight.

For a moment there was no response and then Gwyn laughed. "Down," she said, making Gabe chuckle as well.

"It's actually not funny," said Eddie, stopping dead in his tracks – a fact that Gabe only realized when his face connected with Eddie's solid back.

"I'm not making a joke," Gwyn said, and Gabe realized she'd stopped as well. "I'm stating a fact. The path slopes down."

"You don't have to laugh at me," Eddie said, sounding both injured and annoyed.

Another long pause hung in the darkness, and Gabe could almost feel Eddie's fear and rage bubbling up.

"Eddie," Gwyn said, and Gabe could hear that she was choosing her words very carefully. "It's been a long day. It's going to be a longer night. The sooner we get out of this – whatever it is – the better."

"She's right," Gabe said, trying to calm Eddie even as part of him wanted to shout and scream as well. For a moment, Gabe wished that Merry was there with her quick wit and easy smile.

Eddie drew in a long, shuddering breath and again Gabe had that sense of being able to feel him fighting for control of his feelings. Could it be that not being able to see was enhancing Gabe's other senses? "I know," Eddie said, "but –"

"We don't have time for this," Gwyn stated firmly, and Gabe could hear her normal impatience beginning to reassert itself. "You've got a lot to deal with – I understand – but we need to go. We've got a book to keep safe and my pa to save. Winterfest draws nearer with every breath."

"To save your pa, we need to get to my father," said Eddie, not moving, even though Gabe could feel Gwyn tugging at the cord that kept them together. "Even Lucien said it: we need to go straight to Callchester, to the castle."

"No!" Gwyn's refusal cut hard and fast through the darkness. "That will take too long. You have your letter. Surely that will be enough to convince anyone in Rothwell of who you are."

Gabe felt Eddie take a step forward, and knew he was seeking to touch Gwyn. "It's not," he said, sadly. "Who would we give it to in Rothwell who wouldn't simply burn it? Who can we trust? Everyone who has power there is corrupt! The only one we can convince with this, the only one who matters, is my father. We have to go to him first. Then we can help your father."

"What about the book?" she asked. "The only reason Gabe is here is to keep that book safe."

"The book is safe as long as no one knows I have it," said Gabe.

"They already have Lucien," Gwyn said. "You heard them. How long do you think he will hold out if Ronan decides he wants to torture him for the information?"

"Or Whitmore," Eddie chimed in. "You don't get to be head of the royal personal guard without knowing a trick or two."

Gabe gulped. "Long enough for me to get to Brother Malachy," he said, thinking of the older monk who had been so helpful at Oldham Abbey. "He'll know what to do next."

Gwyn chortled. "So we have two reasons to go straight to Rothwell, and only one to go to Callchester first."

"But it's the strongest reason," Eddie protested. "My father is the most powerful man in this land – even if he isn't well. Once he knows about Lord Sherborne's plot, we will all get what we want, and so much faster than trying to do it ourselves."

"But you're not even convinced your father will recognize you," Gabe said, remembering Eddie's words to Lucien. "Given how unwell he has been. How much time will it take us to convince him of the plot if he cannot lift his head from the pillow?"

Gwyn nodded. "He's right."

"Lucien's letter will convince him – all of them," Eddie said, staunchly. "And you don't even know that your pa is still in Rothwell, remember?" he said to Gwyn. "He'd disappeared from the dungeon last time we looked. And as for Gabe taking the Ateban Cipher straight back to Rothwell . . . the whole point of coming here was to keep it from Lord Sherborne and the Prior. Why deliver it straight back to them?"

"I'd hardly go to Rothwell Castle and hand it over!" said Gabe, stung by Eddie's assessment of the situation.

"You wouldn't need to," said Eddie. "If they got one whiff of the fact you were back in town, you'd be in a dungeon so fast your head would spin. How long do you think you'd manage to keep the book hidden then?"

Gwyn sighed, a sharp, heavy exhalation that carried a world of responsibility within it.

"We need Merry," she said, finally, echoing Gabe's thoughts. "She'll know the best way for us all to get what we want."

"Then let's get to her," Eddie said, finally beginning to move again. "She'll see I'm right, even if you can't."

Gabe followed, one foot in front of the other, his mind whirling. If Merry could come up with a plan that solved all their problems, then she was a miracle worker. Gabe wondered if he'd ever had as much faith in anything as Gwyn had in her sister.

The fact that he suspected not was troubling for someone who had always fully intended to spend his life behind the walls of Oldham Abbey, in prayer and contemplation.

Brother Malachy had always told Gabe that he didn't believe anyone could choose to become a Brother if he had not experienced the world outside, but Gabe had shrugged him off, content with his life and, if he was willing to admit it, scared of what he might find if he stepped outside the gates.

And now, here he was, hundreds of miles beyond not just the gates but his entire home shire, being chased by soldiers, putting his life and the safety of an inestimably valuable book in the hands of a group of girls who had no compunction about stealing for survival – theirs and other people's.

In many ways, Gabe was desperate to get back home – to see Brother Malachy, to try to find an answer to what to do with the Book of Answers, to feel safe again.

But there was a tiny voice inside his head that wondered whether the Abbey was still his home.

A sudden image of Aurora's face filled his mind and he pushed it away. He couldn't think about her now, not here in the uncertain dark, with Oldham Abbey still half a kingdom away.

Taking a deep breath, Gabe squared his shoulders and reached to touch the book reassuringly for the hundredth time that day.

He would focus on what needed to be done and deal with the rest once the book was safe.

After what Lucien had said about the dangers of the book falling into the wrong hands, what else could Gabe do?

CHAPTER FIVE

"Shhh," said Gwyn. "I see a light ahead."

Gabe raised his weary eyes, trying to focus. He felt as though they'd spent days spiraling round and round in the dark, though in reality, it was probably an hour or two at most. Frowning, he was able to make out a faint pinprick of light.

"What is that?" he asked.

"With any luck, it's the end of this infernal ramp," grumbled Eddie. The darkness had definitely brought out the worst in the Prince, who'd muttered and complained and whined throughout the journey. Right up until the point, Gabe remembered with an inward grin, Gwyn had turned and told him that if he didn't pipe down she was going to spin him around and around until he didn't know which way was up and then leave him in the blackness on his own.

Eddie had managed to keep most of his thoughts to himself after that.

"You'll be glad to hear, Your Highness, that I believe it is," said Gwyn, and Gabe smirked when she added in an undertone, "but not more glad than I am.

"The question," Gwyn went on in her normal voice, "is where exactly we're going to end up. If you two can manage not to lose each other between here and there, I'll run ahead and take a look."

"Given there's nowhere to go but forward, I think we can just about accomplish that," said Eddie, but Gabe was relieved to hear a note of humor in Eddie's response. Perhaps the Prince's good nature would return with the light.

Gwyn hadn't even waited to hear a response, dropping the front end of the string and ducking away before Eddie spoke, and it was a minute or two before Gabe heard her excited shout.

"We're here!" she said. "We're –"

The words cut off abruptly and Gabe felt his heart begin to race as he and Eddie, without speaking, began to run towards the rapidly brightening circle of light.

"O-o-h," Eddie said. "Oh, now I see."

Racing up behind him, Gabe was lost for words as he took in the scene.

The tunnel opened up into a huge cavern, light and airy, but completely enclosed. A waterfall splashed down the wall opposite them, landing in a deep, natural pool, and allowing light to spill in with the water droplets through the rocky opening from which it fell. Below Gabe's feet, a stone staircase led down towards a warren of row houses, built against the wall of the cavern, each with a stout wooden door painted in a different bold color.

One pair of wooden doors, three times as large as any of the others, seemed to open into the very wall of the cavern itself.

"What is this place?" Gabe asked.

Eddie spoke without taking his eyes from the scene below, where, Gabe noted, people were beginning to emerge from behind the many doors.

"It's a siege hold," Eddie explained. "Only ancient castles have them. They're designed to provide safe refuge for residents if the castle comes under attack. I think this is why Hayden's Mont looks so . . . abandoned."

"They're all living here?" Gwyn asked. "Why?"

Gabe thought about what they'd seen in the castle – the empty rooms, the cold, the sheer inaccessibility of the castle. "Convenience," he said. "The water is here, I'd imagine that food sources are just beyond those big doors. The slopes of this mountain are inhospitable."

"So they deliver whatever Lucien needs for him and Aurora and he allows them to live in here, out of the snow, safe from the outside world," Gwyn finished, nodding. "Makes perfect sense to me."

And it would, Gabe thought, appeal to Gwyn's innate practicality.

"The question is," Gwyn went on, "are they friendly?"

"We're about to find out," said Eddie as a party of three men detached itself from the small group forming below them and began a determined march up the staircase towards them.

❖

"What took you so long?" Merry's face was fierce even as she pulled Gwyn towards her for a long hug. "I was starting to think that Ronan had grabbed you."

Gwyn snorted, disentangling herself from her sister's arms. "As if," she said. "As far as we know, Ronan and Whitmore are still running around the hallways of the castle trying to work out which way is up."

As far as we know, Gabe thought, glancing over his shoulder at the rapidly disappearing backs of the villagers who had delivered them to Merry.

They'd answered no questions, no matter how hard Eddie had tried to find out more about them. They'd simply stood there in their homespun clothing, their pale faces impassive, and nodded when Gwyn had followed instructions and told them that Lucien had sent them.

Unnerved, Gwyn, Gabe and Eddie had followed when the largest man started down the stairs towards the village, and the other two men had filed down behind them. Halfway down the stairs, Eddie began to pepper the leader with questions about who they were and why they were there, but he hadn't so much as turned a hair to indicate he had heard Eddie's voice.

"I feel as though we're being paraded," Gwyn had muttered to Gabe as they'd reached the rocky floor and continued past the row of houses and the deep pool of water, while a group of grubby children watched, wide-eyed.

"I don't think so," said Gabe, looking around. "I get the feeling they just don't see too many people." He remembered his season serving in the Abbey guesthouse and how astounded he'd been to discover that not everyone in the world wore brown robes. Looking back, he suspected the expression on his face looked similar to those on the children's.

Once at the huge timber doors, Gabe had assumed the silent men would simply turn the key and turf them out onto the slopes outside, but instead the three men had stepped through the doors, indicating they should follow.

Outside, the wind had hit Gabe square in the chest, stealing the breath from his body. One of the men had laughed, brushing his dusty brown hair from his brow, and then re-enacted Gabe's gasp for the benefit of his friends.

Gabe had pulled the cloak of his hood up over his head, shivering, as a forlorn herd of shaggy brown cows stared at him with interest, their mouths moving rhythmically as they chewed over whatever grass they'd managed to forage amongst the rocks. The sky overhead was a pale, leaden gray, tinged with the pink and gold streaks that heralded the dawn, but fat clouds, heavy with snow, hung like fleece around the mountain peak.

Gabe watched the men disappear back into the siege hold with a complete understanding of why they chose to live inside its dusty, dark embrace.

"How did you find us?" Gwyn was asking Merry now, shaking the first flakes of snow from her cloak. "The way I figure it, we're on the other side of the mountain from where we left you."

Scarlett, Merry and Midge exchanged glances. "We had to detour around Sherborne's men," said Scarlett, playing with the end of her braid. "They chased us for a while, but they're old, so they didn't catch us."

Merry laughed. "What she means is that they gave up once they saw that the boys weren't with us," she said. "They're more interested in the book – and Eddie – than they are in us."

Gwyn snorted. "For now."

"Then," said Midge, taking up the story, "I spotted those cows, so we came for a closer look. They're different from any cattle I've ever seen before. Smaller."

"Hairier," Scarlett chimed in, with a shudder.

"But their milk is sweet," said Merry, with a satisfied grin that made Gabe feel very hungry all of a sudden.

"We were just debating whether we needed to come and rescue you when we heard the bells," Midge added.

"And the bells brought those villagers out from their hidey-hole as well," said Merry. "Given that you probably weren't going to escape past Sherborne's men at the front doors of the castle, I had a little feeling that perhaps that hidey-hole was the key. So we decided to wait here."

"Wait for what?" Gabe asked.

"For you, or for the bells to ring again," said Merry, waving her hand towards Hayden's Mont. "I knew it would be one or the other. And if it was the second, that would mean that we'd need to come to the rescue, and we thought we'd have a better chance to do that if we got to know the locals."

"But what about you?" Merry went on without a breath. "What took you so long? Did you deliver the book? Did Lucien endorse Eddie as the Prince? Can we go and save Pa now?"

Gwyn sighed. "Not here," she said. "It's a tale with a lot in the telling and while I think that Ronan will be a while yet, we need to put as much distance between him and Gabe as we can."

"Gabe?" Merry asked. "But surely the book is safe now?"

"Um," Gabe said, drawing the book out from the waistband of his breeches and proffering it towards Merry, who rolled her eyes.

"I see," she said, dusting her hands together. "Well, then, we'd best be off."

She turned to the horses, which were huddled together against the wind, before looking back over her shoulder at Gabe.

"But I'll be waiting to hear that tale."

❖

Sunshine. Warm soup. Hot, glowing coals.

"Stop daydreaming, Sandals," came a sharp voice, breaking into Gabe's reverie. "You're supposed to be steering this horse."

Shaking his head to try to wake himself up, Gabe sat up straighter on Jasper's back. "Sorry," he said. "I was just . . ."

Trying to warm myself up from the inside, he finished mentally, not wanting Gwyn to laugh at him. They'd been traveling back towards Rothwell for weeks now, long enough for the bleak countryside around Hayden's Mont to dissolve into woods and rolling hills.

But the cold was following them, like a faithful dog at its master's heels. It was as though they were bringing winter home with them, and Gabe could see the brutal reality of that in Merry's face.

The cold meant winter, and that meant Winterfest.

For the residents of Rothwell, Winterfest was a chance to get together to celebrate the turn of the season and, most years, the fact that a bountiful harvest had been put aside to see out the long days and nights ahead.

From what Gabe had seen on the way to Hayden's Mont, however, this year's festival would not be a cheerful one for most of the residents of Lord Sherborne's large shire. The tumbledown villages outside of Rothwell had a tired, lackluster feeling, the people stared at them with blank, hungry eyes as they passed and the fields around the cottages were barren patches of dark soil.

Merry, of course, had made a point of talking to people everywhere they went and the stories were all the same. Lord Sherborne had upped the taxes to the point where entire family harvests were taken – and even then, he wanted more.

"They have nothing but debt to look forward to in the springtime – if they last that long," Merry said, bristling with fury. "He has stripped them of everything. On orders from the King."

Eddie was also furious. "This is not the way of my father," he said. "The King has not ordered this. My father sent me to Rothwell to find out why Sherborne has not paid taxes for the past two years – we are receiving nothing from this shire. You cannot blame my father for this – ask Lord Sherborne what he is doing with the money!"

Scarlett sniffed. "I blame the entire tithing system," she said. "These people work hard their whole lives, and can't even feed their families properly. That's why –"

A hard glance from Gwyn stopped her words. Eddie had not seen the girls in action, helping the poor of their villages by robbing the rich who passed by on the Rothwell Road, and as far as Merry and Gwyn were concerned he never would.

Which wasn't to say that Gwyn hadn't been busy on their journey.

"Why what?" Eddie asked.

"Oh, er, why I ran away from home," Scarlett mumbled, staring at her feet.

There was a pause. "I thought that was to avoid marrying that old man on your father's wishes," Eddie said.

"Well, yes, that," Scarlett said, twirling her hair, a deep flush of red spreading up her face. "But the other stuff as well."

Gabe saw Merry's face was also going bright red as she tried to suppress the giggles threatening to explode at the very notion that beautiful, spoiled Scarlett would have left the comforts of home over the plight of the poor.

Gabe had had trouble keeping a straight face himself.

But not now, he thought, shifting uncomfortably on Jasper's back. The movement brought momentary ease to his aching thighs, but it took only a moment before the dull throbbing began again.

With the specter of Ronan and Whitmore chasing them, and the scheduled date of their pa's hanging looming before them, Merry and Gwyn were driving themselves, their friends and the horses to the limits.

Which meant long, painful days in the saddle.

On the bright side, Gabe thought, trying to keep his own spirits up, there'd been no sign of Ronan and Whitmore. He could only hope that they were still busy, searching every nook and cranny of the castle for the Ateban Cipher, which rested in its pouch in the small of Gabe's back.

Merry had gently tried to suggest that he could probably put it in Jasper's saddlebag, but Gabe had simply shaken his head. The last time he'd been separated from the book, he'd watched in horror as its hiding place had been consumed by flames. In that instance, Gwyn had moved the book without Gabe knowing, but he would never forget the sick despair that had consumed him as he'd watched the fire.

And he hadn't even been the designated keeper of the book then.

"We'll stop at the next village," Merry called from her position at the back of the group. Borlan, Midge and Eddie took the front of the line, keeping the big stallion happy, while Bess, Merry's mare, was more than content to plod along behind, though Gabe suspected that Merry chose that position not for the mare's benefit, but for her own. She knew that the chances of a surprise attack were more likely to come from behind them than in front at present, and she kept her bow strung across her saddle, ready for any sign.

"I'm going to give Borlan his head," Midge said. "He's been desperate to run for miles, so we'll meet you there."

Before Merry could respond, the huge horse was gone, cantering down the road at breakneck speed, with Midge and Eddie whooping and laughing on his back. Gabe smiled, and patted Jasper's neck, pleased that the horse maintained his own sedate pace.

"We could give him a kick, put him through his paces," Gwyn said, wriggling as she searched for a more comfortable position behind Gabe.

"He's tired," said Gabe, ignoring the hope in her voice. Gwyn sat as lightly in the saddle as she did most things, but Gabe, while more competent now than he had been when they'd set out all those weeks ago, would never choose to ride when he could walk on his own two feet.

And he would certainly never choose to canter.

"All right," Gwyn groaned, "have it your way. Only we're going to be out here in the cold a lot longer if we don't get a move on."

Gabe considered. "We could take him up to a trot," he said, reluctantly.

"Hallelujah," Gwyn sighed, digging her heels into Jasper's chestnut flanks. "Hopefully, we'll make it before dark."

Behind them, Gabe could hear Bess's hooves pick up the pace as well. As he rose and fell in the saddle in tandem with Jasper's pace, he could feel every bruise on his thighs and his seat begin to throb with the rhythm. Gabe knew that he was going to be sliding off Jasper's back like a sack of barley that night. Again.

❖

Faint pinpricks of light glowed in the dark like the fireflies that lit up the woods around Oldham Abbey in the summer. As he rode into the village, Gabe counted seven cottages in the cluster, with two more lights shining faintly farther back in the dark, indicating a farm or small holding.

"Where's Midge?" Merry said, riding up beside Gwyn and Gabe. "She should be here."

Gabe peered about, but there was no sign of Midge or Eddie, or, more worryingly, of Borlan. A horse that size was hard to hide.

"Maybe they've ridden through to find a camping spot?" Gabe asked, but Merry shook her head.

"Not without meeting up with us first," she said, scanning the sky. "Can anyone see Albert?"

The big bird had been lazily looping over their heads all day, swooping off in search of prey, only to return an hour or two later. Gabe liked to think that he was checking in on Midge. In the early days of their journey, Albert had once tried taking up his customary spot on Midge's shoulder, but Borlan had bucked and whinnied, almost throwing Eddie and Midge to the ground. Gabe had heard Midge talking to Albert later, explaining at great length why he couldn't do that anymore, and smiled to himself. But Albert never tried it again.

"Over there!" said Scarlett, pointing towards one of the lights gleaming farther back in the trees. "See him?"

Gabe followed her finger and saw Albert, wings stretched, backlit by the rising moon.

He glanced over at Merry, who was frowning. "What's Midge doing all the way over there?" she asked, though Gabe had a sense Merry was talking to herself.

"Let's go and find out," said Gwyn. "I really need to get off this horse."

As the horses picked their way through the eerily quiet village, the dull lights threw their shadows against the cottages, but the front doors remained firmly shut and not a soul stepped outside.

"Welcoming place," remarked Gwyn in Gabe's ear.

"It is dark," Gabe reminded her. "There are not many who will open their doors to strangers on a cold winter's night."

"Let's just hope there's an empty barn nearby, then," Gwyn said, with a yawn. "I really don't fancy sleeping on the ground tonight."

As they rounded the last cottage, the empty road stretched ahead of them once more.

"I think we're going to need to go across the fields," said Merry, looking up once again to check Albert's location.

"Dangerous for the horses," Gwyn observed.

"Maybe," said Merry, "but I am not leaving them. There may not be a soul here willing to welcome travelers, but that's not to say they won't take our horses to their hearts."

She slid off Bess's back and, taking up the reins, began to lead the horse through a gap in the hedgerow. "Do you want me to get off?" Gabe heard Scarlett ask as they disappeared behind the greenery.

"You're less of a liability where you are," Merry's voice floated back, and Gabe heard Gwyn suppress a snort.

"You stay there too," she said to Gabe, slithering to the ground and taking Jasper's head to follow her sister. "The fewer people we have falling down rabbit holes, the better."

"I'd rather walk," Gabe said, suddenly desperate to dismount and stretch his legs.

"Well, I'd rather be back in the oak tree eating roasted pheasant," said Gwyn, matter-of-factly, walking as surefootedly across the weed-choked field as though she were strolling the cobbled streets of Rothwell. "But, you know what they say, needs must. Now, pipe down, Sandals, and let me concentrate on getting the three of us wherever we're going in one piece."

After that, Gabe could only allow himself to be led along in silence, listening to the horse's snorting breath in the cold night air, and the rhythmic crunch of his hooves on the frosted earth.

An owl hooted in the woods, probably spooked by Albert's constant, menacing silhouette, but other than that, Gabe heard no sound.

"It's awfully quiet," he whispered to Gwyn.

"Shhhh," she said, and Gabe stiffened, realizing that she was on high alert. "I don't like this at all. Merry, stop."

Ahead of them, Merry froze where she was, asking no questions.

"We need to hide," said Gwyn. "We're sitting ducks out here in the middle of the field – get over to that side, against the hedge."

Merry simply moved, and Gabe again felt that envy well up in him at the trust the two shared.

"Sandals, your wish is granted – get off the horse, get down low and make for the hedge as quick as you can," said Gwyn.

Gabe tried to swing his left leg across Jasper's back, wincing at the knife points of pain that shot up and down his thigh.

"Come on," hissed Gwyn. "Surely even you can manage a dismount."

Stung, Gabe used both hands to lift his leg into position before flinging himself from Jasper's back, landing with an *oof* in the cold, hard dirt.

"Graceful," was all Gwyn said before she and Jasper strode off into the rapidly gathering dark, leaving Gabe alone. He quickly realized he wasn't going to be able to stand up, and rolled over onto all fours instead. Pushing up, he rocked himself back onto his heels, managing to get himself upright.

Gritting his teeth, Gabe began the delicate process of putting one foot in front of the other, gingerly following the path in the frost blazed by Gwyn and Jasper.

"Get down!" Gwyn's voice came at him out of the dark like a punch. "You're not promenading! Crouch!"

Gabe groaned as he bent double, following her instructions – and was glad he had when an arrow whistled over his back, close enough to ruffle his hair!

"Get down!" Gwyn shouted, but this time Gabe didn't need her instruction – he'd already hit the ground, all thoughts of his aching muscles forgotten.

"Merry!" Gwyn shouted again, and Gabe was surprised to hear Merry's voice respond from much farther down the field – back where they'd come from.

"On it!" she said, as another arrow flew over Gabe's prone form, landing with a hard thud in the ground just beside his head.

"Move!" shouted Gwyn, and Gabe crawled on his belly like a lizard, desperately scrabbling towards the hedge. He chanced a quick glance up but could see no sign of any of the girls – or the horses.

Almost sobbing as another arrow landed perilously close to his leg, Gabe dropped his head again, redoubling his efforts as his arms and legs screamed with pain.

Reaching the thick green hedge, he rolled under it with relief, pleased to feel the book pressing hard against his back.

"You okay?" Scarlett's upside-down face peered in at him, and it took Gabe a moment to realize that she was standing on the other side of the hedgerow, fully screened from the bowman by the dense foliage. Poking his head out from under the hedge, he saw she was holding the reins of two horses.

"How did you get them here so quickly?" he asked in amazement, rolling out from his hiding spot and almost landing on her feet.

"Gwyn," she said. "She spotted a gap in the hedge and went straight for it. I just followed with Bess."

"Where is she?" he asked, spitting out dirt. "Where's Merry?"

"Merry went that way," Scarlett said, pointing to the road. "To get a better shot at the archer. Gwyn went that way." She pointed at the light they'd been heading towards. "To see if the bowman has Midge and Eddie."

Scarlett paused. "I'm suspecting he doesn't though," she said thoughtfully.

"Why's that?" Gabe asked.

"Because Albert is still up there," she said, pointing to the moon. "If whoever's shooting arrows at us has Midge, he'd also have the wrath of Albert upon his head . . . And you know what that looks like."

Gabe nodded, remembering Albert's swooping attack on the men who'd set fire to the oak tree.

"We should help them," he said, painstakingly getting to his feet.

"Frankly, I'm not sure you'd be much help right now," said Scarlett, patting him on the shoulder. "Plus, Gwyn told me that we should wait here and –"

A sudden scream pierced the air, high and shrill, making Gabe jump, even as he realized it was coming from the direction Gwyn had taken.

"What was that?" Scarlett whispered.

"I don't know," Gabe said, as the scream was followed by the sounds of a loud scuffle, "but I'm not standing here, wondering. Stay here."

Gabe didn't wait to hear her protests, instead running along the hedge as far as he could before rolling under it and into the field once more. Scrambling to his feet, he ran towards what was clearly a fight, marveling at the fact that he couldn't even feel his legs anymore.

Bursting through foliage, Gabe discovered two figures rolling on the ground, punching and gouging as they hurled indecipherable insults at one another.

He recognized one as Gwyn, and the other was almost as slight, but had dark hair. For one startled moment, Gabe stood and stared at the pair of them, unsure how to even begin to disentangle them.

"Ah," said Merry, strolling up beside him. "I see that Gwyn found the archer."

"Should we . . . ?" Gabe waved a hand at the wrestling figures.

"No, I think she has it in hand," Merry said, flopping down on a nearby log to watch proceedings. "Give her a moment or two."

Sure enough, within moments, Gwyn had rolled her opponent onto his stomach and was sitting on his back, casually tying his hands and feet together with his own belt. It was only when the boy looked up to hiss at her that Gabe realized he was, in fact, looking at a face he knew.

Albeit, the female version of a face he knew.

"Excuse me," he said, trying to gain the attention of the angry, writhing creature. Gwyn stood up and frowned at him.

"Excuse you what?" she asked.

"Well, I just wanted to . . ." Gabe stepped back as the girl on the ground spat at his boots.

"Er, do you know Nicholas?" he asked. "Nicholas who was at Oldham Abbey?"

The girl went still, her pixie face cold and wary.

"Who's asking?"

"I'm Gabe," he responded, feeling a peculiar mix of relief and excitement spread through him. Her response told him that she did know Nicholas, that she probably was in fact his cousin or his sister or some other close relation, which didn't surprise him given the family resemblance. "Nicholas is my friend."

"Oh," she said, breathing out hard. "They said you'd be coming but then, when you were all creeping across the fields like that, I thought –"

"You thought what?" asked Merry.

"Perhaps you'd like to untie me and I might tell you," said the girl, bucking against her restraints.

"Do you promise not to try to shoot us again?" asked Gwyn, arms folded.

The girl gave Gwyn a sharp look. "Well, I won't shoot them," she said. "You, on the other hand . . ."

There was a pause and then, to Gabe's surprise, Gwyn laughed, that deep rich sound that was always so enchanting because it was so rare.

"Fair enough," Gwyn said, reaching down to untie the girl and then help her to her feet. "I'd say the same."

The two stood appraising each other in the pale moonlight for a moment before the girl stuck out a hand. "I'm Camilla," she said. "Cam. You fight pretty good."

"Gwyn," said Gwyn, shaking Cam's hand. "And better than you."

Cam hooted with laughter. "The element of surprise is always a winner. Some other time we might go round again – when we're both expecting it."

"Maybe," said Gwyn, a small smile on her lips.

"Cam?" interjected Gabe. "Nicholas often spoke of a Cam, but I assumed . . ."

Cam laughed again. "You assumed I was a boy," she said. "When Nick went off to the Big House I had to step up to help Papa. We were ever so glad to have him back."

"Nicholas is here?" Gabe said, feeling a huge smile spread across his face.

"Well, yes," she said. "That pinched-up Prior sent him back over some horse or other – that one in the barn, I'd reckon. Near broke my ma's heart it did, but Pa and I told her that it was obviously the Lord's will that he stay here and help with the farm in these bad times, so she's okay with it now."

Merry, Gwyn and Gabe exchanged glances, realizing that Nicholas's prediction had borne true and that he'd been punished over the loss of Borlan and the other horses from the Abbey when he'd helped Gabe to escape.

"That horse in the barn," Merry probed at the point that interested her most, "it came with two riders?"

"It did," confirmed Cam. "Nicholas recognized the horse in the village. We were on our way home from the well with Delphine."

"Delphine?" Gabe asked, trying to keep up with the girl's expanding story.

"Our carthorse," Cam said. "It was getting on dark and we were in a hurry, but then he spotted the horse and dropped the last bucket all over the road."

Cam paused a moment and Gabe could tell she was reliving her own frustration at the dropped bucket.

"He stepped out in front of that big stallion like a madman," Cam continued. "I thought he was going to die, but instead the horse stopped in his tracks and started nuzzling at Nick like a puppy."

She paused again, shaking her head, before focusing on Gabe again.

"We left word for you in the village. Clarry the blacksmith swore black and blue he'd keep an eye out for you and tell you where to go. Wait till I talk to him about this."

"There was no one in the village," said Merry. "No one to be seen anyway. They all seemed to be hiding."

Cam sobered. "They are," she said, with a sigh. "I should have realized when night began to fall. I hadn't realized how far behind you would be."

"To be fair," Merry said, "we didn't know we were expected, and Borlan is *very* fast."

Cam frowned. "Yes, I can see that," she said. "Anyway, you're here now so let's get you up to the barn and then we can –"

"Wait a minute," said Merry. "Who are they hiding from? The villagers? Who did you think we were that you felt you needed to pepper us with arrows?"

"Oh, that," said Cam, already walking away into the dark. "The Black Knights. But let's not talk here. We need to get indoors before they come."

"I'll go and get Scarlett and the horses," Gwyn said, exchanging puzzled glances with her sister. "The sooner we find out what's going on here the better."

CHAPTER SIX

Gabe could hardly keep his eyes open. His belly was full, his body was warm, and the dancing flames seemed to be telling him it was time for bed.

"Don't go to sleep, Sandals," warned Gwyn, with a sharp poke to his ribs. "We've got things to do."

Yawning, Gabe sat up straighter, and tried to focus back in on the conversations flowing around him.

They'd been holed up in the cottage's tiny kitchen for over an hour, while Nicholas's mother, Annwen, fussed over them and fed them a rich beef stew, much to Gwyn's delight. Annwen had noticed Midge politely picking the diced carrot and turnips out of the delicious gravy and made her a simple omelet, bursting with herbs, and soon everyone was full.

Watching Annwen bustling around her kitchen, slender and red cheeked in her simple pinafore with checked apron, Gabe couldn't help but compare her to the sad-eyed woman at Hayden's Mont. If Gabe had ever thought about having a mother – and he hadn't often – then Annwen was close to what he'd imagined: capable, warm and loving.

Midge seemed to feel the same way, and Gabe could hear her now, talking to Annwen about the reading lessons that he had been giving the girls as part of their daily routine on the road. Early in their journey, during one of the long nights, Merry had asked Gabe and Eddie to teach the girls their letters. Eddie had long lost patience with the process, but Gabe had stuck it out, particularly when the girls had proven so quick to grasp the basics.

All the girls except for Midge, he acknowledged, listening as his friend told Annwen how difficult she was finding it. Gabe could picture her now as she had been that very morning, bent over, painstakingly tracing letters in the dirt. He'd wondered then if it was the fact that Midge was the youngest that held her back . . . but he'd begun his lessons around the age of seven – four years younger than Midge was now.

It just seemed that Midge, for some reason, didn't see the letters the same way that the others did.

The older woman patted Midge's shoulder. Gabe couldn't hear what she said next, but it bolstered Midge's confidence, and she sat up straighter, set her shoulders and nodded. The exchange was enough for Gabe to see why Nicholas had gone to Oldham Abbey just to please Annwen.

Gabe couldn't imagine ever doing anything just to please Aurora, who hadn't even recognized him for himself, but as a copy of his father.

Better that he should never have known she existed than to be teased by the idea of what might have been.

"Are you all right?" Midge asked him now, creeping over to take his hand in a comforting gesture.

"Just tired," Gabe had said, unable to put his thoughts into words. And even as he'd spoken, that huge wave of weariness had crashed over him . . .

But now, with the dinner dishes washed and stored neatly away, it was time for business.

"Every few nights they come through Havenmill," Nicholas was saying, his eyes filled with worry. "Ever since I've been back here. Pa says only since then." He turned to his father, a larger, taciturn sunburned version of Nicholas, who nodded his affirmation.

"So only since we've been gone from the Abbey," said Merry, pacing the room, while Gwyn sat silently next to Gabe, as though absorbing every detail through her very skin.

"Yes," said Nicholas. "Always six of them, always after dark, and always dressed in black."

"They told Clarry they were the King's soldiers," Cam piped up. "When he asked them once, that's what they said. And then they cuffed him about the head with a stick for his troubles."

Eddie stiffened at her words though he said nothing. Gabe had seen him and Merry in whispered conference not long after they'd arrived, and could only surmise that Merry had told Eddie not to let on who he was.

"But what do they want?" asked Gabe.

"Destruction," said Nicholas, morosely. "They burn buildings, kick in doors, stop people on the road and steal their money. And there's nothing we can do."

"I'd like to shoot an arrow or two in them, that's what I'd like to do," said Cam, fiercely, her eyes bright with anger and tears. "They burned Goodwife Redmond right out of her home and for what? Because she didn't have enough food in the larder to feed them."

Merry stilled. "Is that so?" she said, slowly.

"Yes," said Cam, her voice shrill with indignation. "Clattered off on their huge horses shaking their fists and carrying on, and then crept back later that night, over the fields . . ."

"Ah," said Merry. "Hence your keenness to put an arrow in us earlier tonight."

Cam blushed, and nodded. "I really thought you were them," she said. "Pa won't talk to them when they come round asking questions – it's hard to tell them that he doesn't talk to anyone much." Her voice trailed away.

"I get the sense they're looking for something," said Nicholas, into the silence. "Or someone. They keep asking about strangers. We don't get too many of them around here – unless you count the Black Knights."

Gwyn sat up straighter. "Every few nights, you say," she said, thoughtfully, and Nicholas nodded.

"They're looking for us," Gwyn said, turning to Merry. "Up and down the main road. That's why they're only passing through here every few nights. They must have a loop north and south."

"Which means they know we headed north," said Merry, considering. "But they don't know how far we went or whether we got there."

"Which means," Gwyn said, "that Whitmore and Ronan are still far enough behind us not to have gotten a message to them yet."

She paused, and Gabe shivered at the look in her eyes. "Are you thinking what I'm thinking?" Gwyn asked Merry.

"I suspect I probably am," agreed Merry, her red curls dancing.

"Er, what are you thinking?" Nicholas asked, looking worried.

"It's time to kill two birds with one stone," said Gwyn, rubbing her hands together. "We'll put a hole in Ronan's army, and bring some peace back to the village at the same time."

"Hopefully," Merry chimed in, "we might even manage some . . . compensation for Goodwife Redmond as well."

Looking at their enlivened faces, Gabe felt his own heart sink at his sudden clear memory of lying on the Rothwell Road, trussed up like a turkey, as the girls did some "fundraising" for a widow from a hamlet near Featherstone. Then, the soldiers involved had been sent packing back to Rothwell, one with an arrow in his ankle.

Gabe had a bad feeling that the Black Knights might fare a whole lot worse.

❖

"Are you ready, Gabe?" Merry said, her whisper seeming to come from nowhere, so dark was the night. "All you have to do is to pull the rope when Gwyn gives the signal. That's it."

Gabe breathed out, trying to relax his tense shoulders, before he answered. "Okay," he said. "I'm ready."

"One job, Sandals," came Gwyn's taunt from the other side of the road. "Mind you don't mess it up."

Stung, Gabe didn't respond, though he grasped his end of the rope more firmly. He still didn't agree with everything that Merry and Gwyn did, but he'd been with them long enough to know that everything they did came from a good place. What they didn't seem to realize was how much Gabe had changed in the weeks they'd been together.

Inside Oldham Abbey, it was easy to know what was right and what was wrong, but he'd soon realized that life on the outside was a lot . . . muddier. As he'd discovered, standing up to evil and bad deeds sometimes took more than words.

Not that he wouldn't always choose words first.

As they waited in the silent darkness, Gabe thought wistfully of Merry's spare bow, wishing that she had trusted him with it. He'd been working hard on his aim whenever possible during the journey, and these days hit his targets more often than not.

But she hadn't so much as glanced in his direction, instead giving the bow to Scarlett, who'd preened like one of Lord Sherborne's peacocks. Merry had answered Gwyn's questioning frown with a shrug, but Gabe had the sense that she was testing Scarlett.

And what a test it might prove to be.

Merry had arranged them on either side of the rutted road, choosing a spot thick with brambles to the north of Havenmill – as always, a spot where the curve of the road gave her the advantage of surprise. The thick length of rope lay between them, Gabe on one end, Gwyn on the other. Merry and Scarlett had taken mirror positions a little farther along the road on Gabe's left, while Cam was hidden in the bushes to his right, with her bow primed. Nicholas was waiting on the other side of Havenmill to perform a very special task.

Midge sat behind Gabe, crooning to Albert, who was perched on her arm, hood in place to keep him quiet.

"Shhhh," hissed Gwyn. "They're coming."

As usual, her catlike ears had picked up the thudding of the approaching horses' hooves minutes before anyone else, but it wasn't long before Gabe heard the soldiers as well, their raucous shouting and ribald laughter carrying clearly on the night air.

"They've been to the Fox," Cam declared in a stage whisper.

"Shh!" said Gwyn.

"Oh, shh yourself," Cam continued, "they're not going to hear anything over their own silly jokes."

Gabe suppressed a chuckle as he imagined Gwyn's face. She was so used to everyone doing what she wanted that it would be interesting to see what she did next.

"What's the Fox?" Gwyn asked, conversationally, to Gabe's surprise.

"Tavern in the next village," said Cam. "It's the only one for miles around."

There was a pause. "Perhaps you'd like to go over there and announce our trap to the whole bar," hissed Gwyn. "You might as well with the amount of *noise* you're making."

There was a small pause before Cam said, "There's no need to be like that. I'll be quiet."

"Then we can be thankful for small mercies," Gwyn said, and Gabe could almost hear her rolling her eyes.

After that, there was nothing to do but wait. The *clip-clop* of the horses' hooves suggested that the soldiers were taking no chances on the uneven road in the pale moonlight, content to swap stories about their various attempts to woo the Fox's serving maids as they plodded along, clearly expecting no challenge that night.

"They're not looking for us now," Midge observed, for Gabe's ears only.

"They're also not moving fast enough for our rope to have an impact," said Merry, appearing next to Gabe like a wraith. "Midge, can you send Albert over to harry those horses?"

Midge nodded. "Leave it to me."

She ducked off into the darkness, and Gabe heard rustling as she moved through the brambles farther north. Gabe wondered what she was going to do, given she'd spent so much time on their journey training Albert *not* to go near the horses.

Within minutes he had his answer, as the horsemen rounded the bend, traveling close together. They'd no sooner loomed into view than Albert shot from the bushes, his screech sounding unearthly as he flew towards the moon. Midge had removed his hood and thrown him up directly in front of the horses, who shrieked in fright, rearing and bucking as the riders desperately tried to control their mounts.

Albert looped around once and then swooped down like a falling arrow, passing within inches of the soldier at the head of the startled group. It was too much for his rearing horse, which landed squarely back on four feet and bolted, the other horses following close behind.

"Steady," came Merry's reassuring voice as the horses hurtled towards them, and Gabe took a deep breath to quell his shaking nerves. The key to this particular plan, Gwyn had explained to him, was timing. Gabe wondered when he'd become more worried about messing up than he was about the right or wrong of what he was doing.

"Not yet . . . not yet . . . not yet . . . NOW!" Merry's command shot through the night, loud enough to be heard over the thudding hooves, screaming horses and shouting soldiers.

Gabe didn't think. His hands tugged hard at the rope almost of their own volition and he felt it strain and tighten at waist height as he pulled. Immediately, he felt a massive pressure and his arms were almost pulled from his body as the lead horse hit the rope, causing it to buckle at the knees, throwing its rider onto the road in front of it. "Let go!" Gwyn shrieked, and Gabe released the rope, feeling it burn his hands as it slithered through them.

To his relief, the first horse was immediately back on its feet, and it continued to trot off down the road; but the damage had been done. The following horses ran into each other, biting and bucking as they tried to shake the riders from their backs and escape.

One by one, the soldiers hit the dirt, cursing and shouting, as their mounts took off towards Havenmill without them. Gabe knew that by now Midge would have run back towards the village to join Nicholas and his father, who'd been tasked with the job of gathering the panicked horses on the other side of town and whisking them off to the warm barn for a soothing bucket of oats and a rubdown.

Within an hour, the horses would be gone, on their way to the girls' home village near Featherstone, where, as Merry put it, a man they knew would know what to do. Gabe suspected it was the same man who'd purchased the carriage horse the girls had "acquired" on the Rothwell Road that first day he'd been with them.

Merry had promised that half the proceeds would be returned to Havenmill to help Goodwife Redmond rebuild and the tenant farmers to eat through winter. The other half would help those suffering in the girls' hamlet.

"Get up!" Merry's voice came from the shrubbery once again, and the dazed soldiers on the road got slowly to their feet. Picking up the end of his rope once more and pulling the hood of his cloak up to mask his face as much as possible, Gabe knew that they had only moments before the men got over the shock of their falls and tried to retaliate – but Merry didn't wait that long, shooting three arrows in quick succession towards the group, landing them almost on the toes of three soldiers, who stepped back to huddle with their friends.

"NOW!" Merry said, and Gabe and Gwyn ran in unison towards the group of men, the thick rope between them. Gabe hoped he could pull this off, remembering watching from up a tree as the girls had rescued him from Sheriff Ronan with the same trick he was about to try.

They passed on either side and then Gabe crossed the road, as Gwyn did the same, pulling the rope in a tight circle around the men. Back and forth they went, crossing over, as the men hissed and cursed, trying to break free of the rope – while Merry, Scarlett and Cam rained arrows around them.

Ducking as an arrow from Scarlett's direction whisked too close to his head, Gabe could only hope that Merry knew what she was doing in entrusting Scarlett with the bow. But he had no time to think further as Gwyn indicated it was time to tie off the rope.

This, he'd been told, was the most dangerous part of the whole operation as they had to get close enough to the struggling men to create a useful knot. Gabe was pleased to see they'd done their work well, with the men's arms pinned to their sides.

"Why can't we just kill them?" Cam had asked when they'd been discussing the plan earlier. "They'd kill us, you know."

"We don't kill unless we have to," Merry had said, once again making Gabe wonder if the girls had ever "had to." But then Merry had winked at him, and he'd felt better. She was clearly just teasing the younger girl. Wasn't she?

"Besides," Merry had continued, "I want them to deliver a message."

And now it seemed the time had come for the message to be conveyed, as Merry, Cam and Scarlett stepped out from the brambles, their hoods covering their hair and most of their faces. Merry kept her face angled down as she strode towards the men, an arrow nocked, its sharp point aimed at the heart of the biggest, meanest soldier. As she swaggered down the road, Gabe realized she'd affected the slouching walk of a youth, quite different to her usual light, balanced gait, and he understood that the men watching her would have no idea she was a girl.

Scarlett, he noted, stayed farther back in the darkness, though her bow was obvious enough, and Cam was simply a silent shadow, albeit a deadly looking one.

While the men were distracted by the new arrivals, Gwyn took the opportunity to tie off the rope in a complicated knot. Gabe noticed that she'd made sure to crisscross the ends of the rope through the center of the huddle before she did so.

To Gabe's surprise, she then pulled her crossbow from under her cloak and aimed it directly at the head of the nearest soldier, who began to whimper.

"Tie their hands behind their backs," Merry said, her voice pitched lower than usual, but raised to be heard above the cursing soldiers. "Starting with him."

She nodded towards Gwyn's captive and tossed Gabe a handful of short, stout pieces of rope. Doing as he was told, Gabe quickly pushed the man's hands behind his back, reaching awkwardly into the huddle behind him to lash his wrists together. It wasn't easy given how squished together the soldiers were within their rope bindings.

As soon as he'd finished, Gwyn moved her crossbow to the next soldier's head, and Gabe followed with the rope.

By now, Merry was talking to the big dark soldier at the front, whose cruel mouth was twisted into a sneer. "You'll be sorry for this," he said, spitting at Merry, who neatly sidestepped the glob of mucus. "You don't know who you're dealing with. We're here on orders of the King." He puffed out his chest as best he could within the tight binds, and Gabe could see a tattered white wolf pinned to his black tunic.

"Ah," said Merry, "should we check on that?"

As the soldiers muttered amongst themselves, she turned and whistled, and Eddie stepped from the brambles. "Let's ask the King's son about your orders, shall we?"

The soldiers looked at Eddie and then turned to each other and laughed.

"He's not Prince Edward!" the big man sneered. "Look how's he's dressed! He's not even wearing the wolf like we are." The other soldiers guffawed.

"Silence!" Eddie roared, and Gabe jumped at the authority in his voice. The only other time he'd heard that note in Eddie's voice was when the Prince had stepped into a Grand Melee and ordered it to stop.

The soldiers subsided, suddenly uneasy.

"I am Prince Edward, Crown Prince of Alban," Eddie went on, stalking across the road towards them, head held high, moonlight making his dark hair gleam.

"Potsblitz!" Cam said under her breath at his words.

"You are not members of my father's personal guard," Eddie went on, looking down his nose at the men before him. "Why do you wear the uniform of the chosen few?"

"We, er . . ." the big man at the front stammered as the others moved restlessly around him. "Well, that is to say . . ."

"Well?!" roared Eddie, and even Gabe had a sudden desire to prostrate himself before his friend.

"Whitmore," said a sour-faced man at the back of the group of soldiers. "We work for Whitmore and Whitmore works for the King so we are in the service of the King."

The big man at the front seemed to gain courage from his words. "That's right," he said, standing up straighter. "And you're nobody from nowhere pretending to be the Prince."

"Yeah," said the sour-faced man. "Untie us and we'll see what's really what."

For a moment, Eddie said nothing, simply pacing back and forth before the struggling men. Gwyn fingered her crossbow and Gabe licked his lips, wondering what would happen next.

"You want me to prove I am the Prince?" asked Eddie, and his voice sounded as silky smooth as pulled taffy. Gabe wondered what he was going to do. Surely he wouldn't show these scoundrels his tattoo?

"Yeah," said the big man, chin pushed forward, jaw tight.

Eddie continued to pace while Gabe held his breath, and then, suddenly, the Prince laughed, a soft, mellow sound.

"A Prince *never* proves anything," he said, and the men looked at each other in confusion.

With that, Eddie walked back into the darkness, with everyone left on the road staring after him. Gabe swore he could almost hear the royal trumpets play as Eddie disappeared.

"Right," said Merry, drawing the men's attention back to her. "You saw. You heard. Now, on your way."

"What?" the big man exploded. "Go where? We can hardly walk tied together like this."

"Then you'd best get moving," said Merry, raising her bow to her shoulder once more. "It's a long walk back to Callchester."

With a muttered curse, the man took a few tiny steps forward, while the other soldiers tried to follow, their feet tangling together.

"Don't fall over now," said Gwyn, and Gabe could hear the laughter underlying her words. "You won't get back up again."

The sour-faced man swore viciously at her, bringing a huge smile to Gwyn's face, as she grabbed Gabe's arm, dragging him into the brambles. From their position in the undergrowth, Gabe saw the sour-faced man turn around and stop, looking puzzled. The road behind him was empty and peaceful, the only sign that anything had happened there a churned-up patch of dirt where the horses had reared.

The man turned back to his comrades and muttered something, at which they all tried to pick up the pace, hobbling along like a large, unwieldy multi-legged newt.

"That should do it," Gwyn said in Gabe's ear.

Gabe followed her passage through the brambles as best he could, wincing as the prickly shrubs scraped his skin. On one hand, he could see that they'd done some good here, saving Havenmill from this troublesome band of men, and helping out Goodwife Redmond in the process. But he wondered just how long it would take for news of their exploits to reach Whitmore, who would immediately know (a.) where they were and (b.) that Eddie was still with them.

He sighed, wondering if this was all part of Merry's plan – and if there would ever come a day when he'd be a step ahead of these girls.

CHAPTER SEVEN

"Stay here, our barn is warm and Winterfest draws near. You've done so much for us and it's even more dangerous on the road for you now." Annwen spoke as she tucked a dishcloth into her apron, her concern clear.

Gwyn answered from her position near the fire. "It's more dangerous for us to stay here," she said. "Not for us, but for you. The first place they'll look for us is the last place we were seen and there can be no hint that you've even heard of us."

"Clarry the Blacksmith saw us with Borlan," said Cam, nervously. "We gave him that message for you."

Merry nodded to Gwyn, who stood at once. "I'll speak to Clarry now," she said, moving towards the door. "I think you'll find he remembers no such thing."

She was gone before anyone could respond, and Gabe saw Cam shake her head in astonishment. He hid a smile, knowing how much Gwyn would hate the hero worship that shone in Cam's eyes.

With Gwyn gone, Merry began to pace the floor muttering to herself, and Gabe could see her formulating and discarding plan after plan. Eddie, Midge and Scarlett, used to her ways, talked softly amongst themselves, while Nicholas's family watched on, fascinated – and slightly askance, as though she were transforming into a madwoman in front of them.

Gabe began to run different ideas through his own mind, using her process of logic to come up with – and reject – his own plans. Finally, staring into the flames, he had an idea that, no matter which way he probed at it, seemed not too awful. "Er," Gabe said, standing up to tap Merry on the shoulder.

"What is it?" she snapped, deep in thought.

"I, well, I've got an idea," he said. "I read this book once about a horse that wasn't really a horse – it was a pretend horse, given as a gift, and then there were soldiers hidden in the belly and they took the enemy's castle . . ." His voice trailed away as she stared at him.

"You think we should build a fake horse?" Merry asked, politely.

"Er, no," Gabe said, feeling beads of sweat popping up on his brow as everyone in the room stared at him. "I think we should go to Callchester Castle in disguise. And then, once we're inside we can find the King."

There was a pause. "When you say 'disguise,'" she said, "what would you suggest?"

"Minstrels," Gabe said, turning to Scarlett. "Midge even said one day that Scarlett and I should make some money singing at Winterfest. We often got groups of wandering minstrels at the Abbey guesthouse. We could disguise ourselves like that."

Scarlett pursed her lips. "That might get us into the courtyard," she said. "But we'd need a good reason to get beyond that. I know my father very rarely allowed strangers into the keep at all, let alone into his chambers, and I'd imagine it would be even harder to get to the King."

She turned to Eddie, who was looking doubtful. "What would get us into the solar?" Scarlett asked. "Think, Eddie!"

Eddie exhaled, tapping his foot as he thought. "Lucien," he finally said. "I think that my father has been awaiting a gesture of . . . forgiveness . . . apology . . . from Lucien for years. We can say that Lucien sent us with a special song for him. He won't say no to that."

There was a long pause as Merry considered the idea, a smile playing at her lips. "Well, well, well," she said eventually, her gaze taking in all three of them. "Who'd have thought you had that in you? We'll ride out for Callchester in the morning."

Gabe swallowed. "Oh, about that," he said, not looking forward to her response – or Gwyn's – to his next revelation. "We won't be able to ride."

"This was a really good idea, Gabe," said Merry, and Gabe felt his ears go hot with her praise.

"Oh yeah, just great," muttered Gwyn, shifting her weight beside him, trying to get comfortable. "Let's leave the valuable, fast horses behind with Nicholas and take the slow, plodding carthorse to Callchester. It'll be high summer by the time this fleabag gets to Rothwell, and after that Pa will be dead in the ground."

Merry elbowed her sister. "We agreed that the best time to rescue Pa was Winterfest itself, which is still five days away," she reminded Gwyn. "We also agreed that the best way to rescue Pa was on the royal command of Prince Edward, so it's in our best interests to go to Callchester first. We've got time and we need to stick with the plan."

Gwyn muttered under her breath, but Gabe caught the words "*your* plan, not *the* plan." It had taken a lot of hard talking to finally agree on a course of action, and in the end Merry had agreed with Eddie that seeking his father's help was it. She talked Gwyn around. "It solves Eddie's problem, our problem *and* keeps Gabe and his book away from Lord Sherborne and safe with us," Merry had told her sister. "Eddie's right – we don't even know where Pa is right now!"

"Ignore her," Merry said now, turning back to Gabe. "She's just grumpy she didn't think of it first."

"I like it," said Scarlett, lying full length along the wooden slats of the cart on which they were riding. "At least my, er, seat gets a rest this way. I'm not sure how much longer I could have sat on Bess, to be honest."

Gwyn's *hmmmph* was drowned out by Eddie and Midge agreeing with Scarlett.

"If riding had been the best way to go, that's what we'd be doing, your, er, seat or not," said Merry, with a grin. "But Gabe was right. They'd spot Borlan before they spotted any of us – and they're not looking for a cartload of traveling minstrels."

Gabe could smile now, thinking of the moment he'd told her that groups of wandering minstrels had typically arrived at the Abbey guesthouse squeezed into one cart. But Gwyn's response had been as unhappy as he'd expected – and her outlook hadn't become any sunnier as they bumped along the rutted track at plodding carthorse pace.

"We should sing as we go," Scarlett said now. "That's what real minstrels do. They get more money that way, because people sometimes throw coins at them as they pass through villages."

Gabe patted the lute tucked into the cart beside him, stroking the pear-shaped wooden body before checking that the strings were still intact. The sheep gut was worn in places, but surprisingly strong, given the instrument had been stored away at the back of a dusty cupboard for nigh on twenty years.

Scarlett's sharp eyes didn't miss the gesture. "I thought Nicholas and Cam were going to faint when their father pulled out the lute last night," Scarlett said.

Gabe chuckled. "It was pretty surprising," he said. "But very generous of him to lend it to us for the cause, given it was his own father's."

"I wonder that he never learned to play it himself," Eddie said. "It's a lovely instrument."

Gabe glanced down at it, taking in the sheen of the spruce soundboard, the delicate intertwined vine that made up the carved grille over the sound hole, and the sweet curve of the lute's belly.

"He may not have played it, but he's looked after it," said Gabe. "And lucky for us. A group of minstrels without an instrument of any kind would look suspicious."

"We'll look more suspicious if we actually let Gwyn sing," Merry joked, earning herself a sharp glance from her sister. "But if we put Gabe and Scarlett up front, nobody will even notice the rest of us are there."

Gabe stared at his boots as the wave of heat rose through him again and he could see that Scarlett's cheeks had turned pink as well.

"So now you are the keeper of the lute, as well as the –" Eddie began to joke, but Gabe cut him off with a hard stare, not wanting to even mention the Ateban Cipher in the open cart. He couldn't see anyone hiding behind the dense brambles that lined the road – but that didn't mean there was no one there.

Eddie rolled his eyes. "No one can hear us!" he said. "And even if they could they wouldn't know what we were talking about. You wouldn't even let me mention the word 'book' in front of Nicholas and his family last night."

Gabe paused as the cart hit a particularly deep pothole, jolting them all and causing Gwyn to sigh even louder. "If they don't know, they can't tell," he said, remembering Brother Malachy's words on the very first day that Brother Benedict had handed Gabe the book. "I can't see Nicholas and his family as skilled liars and if Ronan and Whitmore do somehow turn up at the farm, I don't want them to have to fake innocence."

Eddie paused before nodding. "You're right," he conceded. "Whitmore is a skilled interrogator. He would know."

Gwyn snorted, staring down the bumpy road behind them, keeping watch as always. "Well, you'd better hope Ronan doesn't find them then," she said, without looking at Gabe. "Because he won't *care*."

Gabe swallowed, but refused to be baited. He had to believe that Nicholas and his family would be okay, because the alternative was unthinkable – and it would be all his fault.

"They'll be fine," said Midge, reaching over to touch Gabe's arm. "Merry has covered our tracks well and there's no reason for those bad men to even go to their little farm."

Gabe nodded, smiling down into her big, brown eyes. She looked so small sitting beside him, and he was constantly having to catch himself, remembering that she was just as capable as any member of the group – if not more so, with Albert on her shoulder as he was now, tucked away in his hood, into which Midge had stuck a jaunty little white chicken feather. "He looks less mean now," she'd explained to Gabe when he'd found her doing it that morning. "More like he might be a performing bird, part of the minstrel show."

Gabe had suppressed a smile at the thought of the ruthless predator, with his rapacious beak, beady eyes and cruel claws, performing as part of an act, but Midge sincerely believed that her bird was the sweetest creature in the world.

Truth be told, if Midge told him to do backflips and fly through a ring of fire, Albert probably would, Gabe concluded, so maybe she wasn't far off.

"I've been trying to practice my reading on the road signs," Midge continued shyly. "Do you think I'll ever get better, Gabe?"

"I'm sure you will," he said, trying to sound confident, remembering her conversation with Annwen.

"I don't know," she sighed. "It's like I don't remember the letters from one day to the next. Like they just float away."

Gabe opened his mouth to answer, but was distracted by a sudden change in the *clip-clop* rhythm of Delphine's hooves on the stony road. The cart rumbled to a bumpy stop.

"What is it?" asked Gwyn, looking to Midge. "Why has she stopped?"

Midge's uncertainty disappeared as she shifted Albert to perch on the front of the cart and then clambered over Gabe and jumped to the ground, running to Delphine's head, with Merry following.

"Stay there," Merry ordered. "Keep your eyes on the trees around us."

With a gulp, Gabe turned his attention to the tangle of dark trunks and deep evergreen leaves that lined his side of the road. Was this a trap? Merry seemed to think so.

"It's a stone!" said Midge. She had the horse's right foreleg tucked between her knees, and was attempting to pry the offending rock from the hoof with her fingers. "I can't get it loose."

"Let me try," said Merry, and moved towards the horse to try her luck. But Delphine was having none of it, trying to move sideways within the constraints of the cart's shafts.

"I can do it," said Midge, "but I need something sharp to pry under it."

With a sigh, Merry moved back to the cart, pulling one of her arrows from its hiding place beneath the lunch basket. Midge used the sharp, pointed edge to loosen the stone, holding it aloft with triumph.

"There you go, all better," she said, before turning to Merry. "I'll walk beside her for a while until she settles."

Merry climbed back on the cart and Midge urged the horse forward at a slow walking pace. Delphine took one step, then one more before Midge pulled her to a halt.

"It's no good," she said. "She's limping."

"Great," breathed Gwyn. "Not just a slow horse, but a lame horse at that."

"I heard that," said Midge, sharply. "And she can't help it. She's doing her best to get us where we want to go."

Gwyn rolled her eyes, but said nothing more.

"What should we do?" Merry asked, ever practical. "We can't pull the cart ourselves."

Midge frowned, stroking the horse's neck. "I need to wrap the whole hoof," she said. "If I can do that, it might be enough to protect the bruise. But, ideally, I'd apply a salve first."

She stopped, staring into the trees. "Is that wood smoke I smell?"

"Cottage over there," said Gwyn, waving her hand at the trees.

"Where?" Gabe asked, looking from side to side.

"Look up, Sandals," Gwyn said. "See?"

Gabe stared up over the tall, leafy canopy and there it was – a wisp of smoke coming from somewhere behind the wall of trees.

"Has to be a woodsman of some kind, all the way out here," mused Merry. "He'd have something you could use, wouldn't he, Midge?"

Midge nodded. "I think so," she said. "He'd keep something on hand for himself if not for any animals he might have. Comfrey would do it, I'd say, wouldn't you, Gabe?"

Gabe considered for a moment. Comfrey, a herb also known as bruisewort or woundwort, had been used in the Infirmarium on the Brothers and travelers unlucky to injure themselves. "I can see no reason it wouldn't work on a horse," he said slowly.

"Great," said Gwyn. "Then why don't you two pop on over to that cottage to borrow a cup of comfrey."

"You can go too," said Merry, without glancing Gwyn's way, handing Midge a few coins. "A walk in the woods might take the edge off that sour mood you're in."

With a *hmmph*, Gwyn picked up her crossbow, rolled herself over the side of the carriage and stalked off into the woods, Gabe and Midge happy to let her lead the way, once Midge was satisfied that Albert was content where he was.

As they stepped into the tangle of trees, their footsteps were immediately muffled by the thick layer of leaf matter on the forest floor. Gabe breathed in the pine-scented air with pleasure.

"I used to love this time of year," Midge said, quietly padding along beside him. "My mama always filled our cottage with pine boughs for Winterfest." She sighed. "But now it's getting harder and harder to remember even their faces," she said, staring off into the distance as though to conjure up her parents, killed by unnamed soldiers.

"It must be difficult for you," said Gabe.

Midge turned to him, her brown eyes sad. "It is," she said, then hesitated.

"What?" he asked, keeping a close watch on Gwyn who had not so much as glanced behind to make sure they were still following.

"No harder than it is for you," Midge said, placing a hand on his arm. "Gwyn told Merry and me what happened at the castle. I can't imagine what it must feel like."

Gabe said nothing, still unable to put into words what he was feeling about Aurora.

"If you want to talk about it," Midge said, "we're all here to listen."

"What is there to say?" Gabe asked. "I had no mother or father, now I have a mother who is not really a mother, and no father. I don't think much has changed for me really."

"Are you two planning on standing about nattering all day?" asked Gwyn, interrupting their conversation, and Gabe looked up to see her stalking back towards them, the crossbow held lightly in one hand. "The cottage is just there and I'd quite like to get this comfrey and get on our way before Winterfest. You know, to save my pa."

Midge dropped Gabe's hand and took Gwyn's. "We're coming. It will only take a moment to get some comfrey and we'll be back on the road before you know it. We want to save your pa as much as you do."

To Gabe's surprise, Gwyn softened, soothed by Midge's touch.

"I'm sorry," Gwyn said, shortly. "I'm just –"

"Worried," Midge finished, pulling Gwyn along beside her as they walked towards the cottage, still hidden by tree trunks, though Gabe fancied he could now feel the smell of the wood smoke penetrating his hair and clothing, and could definitely hear some chickens clucking. "We know. And we're worried too, so there's nothing to be sorry about."

Gabe let them walk ahead, talking softly, while he followed, hands in the pockets of his breeches, deep in thought.

"Come on, Sandals," Gwyn said, startling him. "Get ready. We don't know what to expect here."

Gabe ran over to join them, glad she'd dragged him out of the morass of his own mind. Gwyn crouched down at the edge of the clearing, indicating the others should follow. "What do you think?" Gabe asked.

"I think you should be quiet," Gwyn said, studying the scene intently.

Gabe did as he was told, eyes roaming over the long, narrow shack, the neatly tended herb garden that lay to one side of it, and the red-brown chickens scratching contentedly in the dirt outside the tightly shut front door. Puffs of smoke chugged out of the smoke hole in the thatched roof, and

Gabe noted with interest a high, sturdy fence behind the cottage, suggesting an animal pen of some kind.

"What do you think?" Midge asked.

"I think you two should go in there and get whatever it is you need and we'll be on our way," said Gwyn. "Don't walk out just here, go through the brambles to the south and step out there."

"What about you?" Gabe asked, as Midge disappeared into the undergrowth.

"I'll wait here," Gwyn said, drawing the string on her crossbow to the firing position and setting a bolt in readiness. "Just in case."

Gabe exhaled slowly and nodded. "Okay," he said, getting up to follow Midge, who was already halfway across the clearing.

"Sandals." Gwyn's loud whisper floated across to him on the breeze. "Keep your eyes open – the slightest hint of anything off and you get Midge out of there."

Gabe nodded without looking back, feeling his shoulders tighten and his mouth go dry. Midge seemed to have no such qualms, however, and was rapping on the front door, the *rat-a-tat* echoing around the clearing and setting the chickens to flight.

By the time Gabe reached her, he could hear soft thumps and a muffled voice from behind the door, followed by a rattle as the latch was lifted and a long creak as the door swung open. Framed in the doorway, pale in the dim interior light, stood a weather-beaten old man, his white beard and hair almost down to his waist, his horny feet bare.

"Yes, what is it?" he asked, and Gabe noted the waver of age in his voice and his red-rimmed rheumy eyes and wondered how he made his way out here all alone in the woods.

"Good morrow, kind sir," Midge said, gently laying a small hand on the man's arm. "Our horse has bruised his foot on the main road and we are hoping to find some comfrey."

"Find?" the man asked with a frown, his voice rising. He reached behind the door and withdrew a stout walking stick.

"Buy," said Midge, reassuringly, and the man relaxed his grip on the stick. "We'd like to buy some comfrey to treat our horse. And a cloth to wrap it in if you have one."

"Ah, now that's a different matter," the man said, sounding relieved, and stepping out onto the porch beside them.

Gabe took a step back as he now saw for the first time the grubby white wolf the man had pinned to his soiled tunic. Midge frowned at him, and continued talking to the man in a pleasant, singsong voice.

"I am . . . Molly," she said, letting Gabe know that she'd also noted the wolf. "And this is –"

"Glen," said Gabe, looking around for inspiration. "I'm Glen. This is a nice place you have here."

The man stared at him suspiciously. "Yes, well don't you be looking too closely at it," he said, before turning to Midge. "Now, Missy, I'll get you your comfrey and you can be on your way." Leaning heavily on the stick, he thumped his way down off the porch.

"Very well," said Midge, following him down the side of the cabin.

"Not him," the man said, pointing the stick at Gabe. "You wait there."

Gabe nodded, understanding why a half-blind old man would feel more comfortable with Midge. Gabe could hear Midge chatting away to him and judged from the sound of her voice that they were in the garden. He glanced down the other side of the cabin, noting that the chicken coop was better tended than the house itself – but not as new as the fence that ran along the back of the cottage.

Curious, Gabe jumped down from the porch and made his way to the fence, admiring its solid construction. It seemed to be built from tree saplings, pointed at both ends, with one end pushed deep into the forest floor.

Running a hand over the rough bark of the saplings, Gabe frowned, wondering how a solitary old woodsman had built such a thing. It reminded Gabe of a drawing he'd once seen in a book about an ancient war – the illustrator was depicting a defensive structure.

Bang! Gabe jumped back in fear as something hit the other side of the fence – hard!

"Oi, you! What are you doing?" The old man was thumping his way towards Gabe, waving his stick.

"I, er, sorry," Gabe said. "I was just admiring your fence."

The man frowned. "Well, don't," he said. "Now be off with you. That little lassie has her comfrey and her cloth and you can both be gone."

"What's behind it?" Gabe asked, curiosity overcoming his instinct to obey. He could just imagine Prior Dismas's response to such a query.

"You see this," the man said, smacking the patch on his chest. "This means I don't have to answer your questions."

"Er, okay," said Gabe, but even as he turned away there was another huge bang on the other side of the fence, shaking one of the saplings until it looked as though it would fall.

"You must have a big horse in there," said Gabe, staring at the fence.

The man laughed. "You might say that," he said. "I'm looking after it for the King."

Gabe glanced at his wolf patch. "Is that why you wear the patch?" he asked, hoping he sounded innocent.

"Yes," said the man, and the word was so full of pride that Gabe knew the man really did think he was working for the King. "A big man came and asked for me especially."

"A big man?" asked Gabe, trying not to appear too interested.

"All in black," the man said, leaning on the stick, happy to be chatty now that Gabe was leaving. "And that other one, the Sheriff, comes by every month or so to pay. Due any day now, come to think of it."

Gabe nodded, recognizing the description of Whitmore and thinking that the "Sheriff" could only be Ronan of Feldham. "You must be very good at your job then," he said, politely, feeling a sudden urge to be away from the cottage. "Thank you for the comfrey."

Gabe shook the man's hand, and took his leave, rushing back to Gwyn to share what he'd just learned. Whatever was on the other side of the fence was something that Whitmore and Ronan of Feldham both wanted hidden. Which meant it was something that Gwyn would want to take a look at.

❖

"The King's stag!"

Following on Gwyn's heels, Gabe could see that she'd startled Merry, barreling out of the trees as she had, breathless with excitement.

"The King's stag!" Gwyn repeated, as Merry stepped towards them. "We found it. Well, Sandals did."

Gabe blushed as Eddie jumped down from the cart. "It's alive?" he asked.

Gabe nodded. "Alive and well, if a little thin and unhappy," he said. "We had to climb a tree to see him."

"*Very* unhappy," said Midge, sounding angry. "He's being kept in a pen, and it looks as though he's been there ever since he disappeared from our forest." She stomped over to Delphine, the carthorse, and bent down to her injured hoof. "Scarlett, can you bring me some water please?"

"But that's horrible," Scarlett breathed, unstoppering a water flask and handing it to Midge. "How could they keep a beautiful wild animal like that cooped up that long? And who's *they*?"

Gwyn glanced at Gabe. "Whitmore," he said quietly. "And Ronan of Feldham."

Merry began pacing. "Whitmore and Ronan," she muttered. "Working together since the stag disappeared."

She stopped suddenly. "This has something to do with Pa!" she declared. "That's why they hid the stag, to give them a reason to hang him."

"But why?" protested Gwyn. "What could he know? What could he have seen? He's a simple woodsman. He'd have told us. Warned us."

Merry wiped her eyes, and Gabe realized she was crying. "He doesn't know," she said, her voice shaking. "He must have been in the wrong place at the wrong time and they think he's seen them together, or he knows something. Maybe he saw them with the boy from the mill – didn't you think that Eddie was him at first? The imposter?"

Scarlett gaped. "They jailed him just in case?"

Merry could only nod as the sisters clung to each other. "All this time . . ." said Gwyn, burying her face in Merry's shoulder.

"And now they're going to hang him, just in case," said Gwyn, stepping back, her voice cold, emotions under control.

"No," said Merry, her eyes glittering. "They're not. Because we know where the stag is and it will help to prove our case."

"Only as long as they don't know we know," said Gwyn. "If they get wind that we know, they'll move it."

Gabe stepped forward. "Ronan is due any day to make a payment to the old man for the stag's keep," he said.

Merry paused. "Should we set it free?" she asked Gwyn. "That way they won't have it either."

Gwyn shook her head. "Sandals, Midge and I talked about that while we were there," she said. "We think it's best to leave it where it is for now. Midge isn't convinced it would find its way back to our forest. We're still several days from Rothwell."

"But the woodsman – will he say something?" Merry asked.

"He's old and he doesn't see that well," said Gwyn. "He'd have no reason to mention us unless Whitmore or Ronan specifically asked if we'd been there. And why would they?"

"No reason at all, unless they see us sitting here by the side of the road," said Eddie, glancing behind them, and Gabe gulped.

"How's the horse?" asked Merry, as Scarlett strolled over to join them.

"Midge is just wrapping the poultice around the hoof," said Scarlett.

"Will she be able to walk?" Gwyn called to Midge, who finished tying a knot and stood.

"The binding will protect the bruise while the comfrey works," she said. "But she'll be tender. We'll have to take it easy for a while."

"Great," muttered Gwyn, but Gabe noted that she followed her sister's lead and jumped up onto the cart.

As Delphine began to plod away, her hooves *clip-clopping* unevenly on the hard-packed dirt, the cart rumbling slowly behind, Gabe tried to force himself to relax, remembering that he was supposed to be a carefree wandering minstrel. But rather than looking ahead, he found himself watching the dusty road behind them. Glancing across the cart, Gabe noticed that Gwyn was doing the same thing.

CHAPTER EIGHT

"Is everyone ready?"

Gabe glanced around the circle, pleased with what he saw. On the surface, at least, and thanks to Gwyn, they looked like a group of wandering minstrels. Scarlett was wearing a long blue gown laced across the front, her hair braided and beribboned, a white mask covering half her face.

Eddie, Merry and Gwyn were all decked out in clean white tunics, their boots lustrous with grease, faces hidden by full masks of the type that court jesters wore. Midge looked angelic in a simple white blouse and skirt, her face bare. Looped over one wrist, she carried a small white drawstring pouch, in which was hidden the Ateban Cipher.

Gabe had given it to her reluctantly, only because his own costume of red hose, blue tunic and matching blue mask left him nowhere to conceal the book. To Merry's amusement, Gabe held the lute across the front of his body, aware that never in his life had so much leg been exposed.

He was feeling the cold fingers of winter through the thin tights.

Gabe had no idea where Gwyn had conjured up such costumes from, but she'd disappeared with Midge soon after they arrived on the outskirts of Callchester, taking her mother's precious teacup with her, and reappeared soon after carrying the armful of clothes.

"We have these for one day," she'd said, handing them out. "After that, they keep the teacup." Her tone suggested there was no way she'd be allowing that to happen, and so their deadline was set.

Now they were gathered on the bustling street outside the imposing gates of Callchester Castle, preparing for the performance of their lives.

"Ready?" asked Scarlett, with a composed smile. She and Gabe and Eddie had practiced a wide repertoire of songs during the journey to the King's castle, and Gabe knew that Scarlett had been gratified by the coins and other trinkets that had rained down upon them as they'd made their way through towns and villages. Merry had gathered up the coins carefully and delivered most of them to the poorest-looking cottage in the next village they'd come to, keeping just a few on each occasion for their own needs.

"As I'll ever be," said Gwyn, and Gabe hid a smile. Of all of them, Gwyn was the most uncomfortable with their plan and Gabe knew that it was mostly because she was happiest going in and out of places in the most inconspicuous manner possible. To boldly arrive at the front gate and demand an audience with the King went against every instinct she had. Added to that was the fact that she would rather face Whitmore on her own than to sing in public. Gabe knew that Gwyn couldn't wait to get this over with and go to collect her teacup.

Merry, Midge and Eddie nodded, and Gabe led the way past market stalls piled high with winter vegetables, salted meats, bolts of fabric and other essentials. They'd left Delphine and the cart in the stable at an inn on the outskirts of town, and Merry had spent the last of their coins to send a message to Nicholas to let him know where the horse was. Eddie had promised that as soon as he was recognized by his father, they would have access to any horse they wanted from the royal stables to gallop to Rothwell to save Ralf Hodges. With just three days to Winterfest, they would need the fastest horses the King had.

Gabe wrinkled his nose as they passed a fishmonger's stall, the whiff of mackerel, herring, lamprey and eels assaulting his senses. A sudden blast of laughter and music suggested that someone had just entered the tavern on the corner, though the door was pulled shut with a bang soon after. Several people warmed their hands around a brazier where a man with red cheeks and twinkling eyes was roasting chestnuts before pouring them into paper cones.

But now they were at the gates, and Gabe's fingers were so stiff and cold that he could only hope he wasn't asked to prove his lute-playing credentials by playing a song on the spot. With a glance behind him to make sure the others were there, Gabe marched over the drawbridge that lay across the wide moat and banged on the big doors.

A small window opened to his right, revealing a strong iron grate.

"Yes." The voice was gruff and hard.

"Er, we're minstrels, here to play for the King," Gabe said.

There was a pause before the window slammed shut.

Gabe stamped his feet, wondering what to do next. "Come on, Sandals," came Gwyn's voice at his shoulder. "You need to do better than that."

Gabe nodded, steeling himself to bang again.

The window popped open. "You still here?" came the gruff voice. "The King is receiving no visitors, and especially not singing ones."

The window began to shut.

"Lucien sent us," Gabe burst out, putting a hand on the grate. "For the King."

There was a pause. "Lucien, you say? What do you know of Lucien?"

"Hayden's Mont," Gabe replied and, as though he'd offered up a magic password, the window slammed shut and a small door concealed within the main gates opened.

"Come on then," said the grizzled guard, the owner of the gruff voice. "Get in here so I can get a better look at you without the whole street wanting to join us."

Gabe smiled as he led the others through the gate, pleased to have gotten over the first hurdle. But once inside the gates, his heart sank, realizing that getting inside the outside gates didn't get them much closer to the King. Instead, they were standing on the cobbled walk between the tall outer walls and the soaring stone turrets that formed the entrance to the gatehouse.

To Gabe's right was another huge corner turret, its narrow windows covered with heavy iron bars.

"The prison tower," Eddie muttered in his ear, his gaze following Gabe's. "To be avoided."

Gabe nodded, and followed the grizzled guard down the narrow walk to the gatehouse, where two other soldiers stood to attention.

"What you got there, Yates?" the taller soldier asked the grizzled guard.

"Minstrels," Yates said. "For the King."

"From what I hear, the King's in no mood for song," said the tall man.

"Rumors," grumbled Yates. "If this castle was fed on rumors, we'd all be fat."

"More than rumors, if you ask me," said the other soldier, leaning on his spear, his long red hair falling like a sheet of flame from beneath his helm. "Willard reckons he heard from Shelton that Whitmore reckons –"

"That'll be enough of that," said Yates, cuffing the man on the arm. "Whatever Whitmore reckons or does not reckon doesn't count round here right now, given he's not been seen for nigh on two months. Now –" He turned his attention to Gabe. "Give us a song."

"Er, what?" said Gabe, who'd been expecting to have to tell his made-up story about who they were and where they were from.

"A song," Yates repeated, as though speaking to a small child. "You do sing, don't you? Being minstrels and all?"

Gabe nodded.

"Yes, well, that's what they all say," said Yates, "and you should have heard the shrieking that came from the last lot we had through here. So, Lucien or no Lucien, I'm not letting you go any farther without hearing you. It's not worth my job."

"Lucien?" said the tall soldier, but Yates cut him off with a withering glance.

"Right," said Gabe, turning to the others. Scarlett and Eddie immediately moved up beside him, standing shoulder to shoulder in an effort to conceal the fact that the other three would be doing little more than mouthing the words. Gabe sang a C note, gratified to hear it echoing in the confined space. The acoustics were good enough that three of them singing would sound much fuller.

He nodded to Scarlett and Eddie and they began to sing. On the cart, they'd decided on a program of five songs, starting with "Once a Fair Maiden," the haunting ballad they'd first sung to mark time in the tunnels under Rothwell Castle. Eddie had told them that his father never listened to more than five songs before paying the minstrels with a gold piece.

"To tell the truth, he doesn't really enjoy the shows at all," Eddie said with a smile. "He'd much rather hunt or fish or just walk about the gardens. But a good King must appreciate the finer things in life."

"Sounds dull to me," said Gwyn. "Sitting around listening to people sing when you could be outdoors."

Eddie had laughed. "I think you and my father would get on very well."

Now Gabe tried to ignore the tuneless humming behind him and concentrated on blending his voice in, over and around those of Scarlett and Eddie. The little goose bumps that prickled their way up and down his arms told him that the sound was good, even if the blank faces of the three guards gave nothing away.

As the last note died away, Gabe caught Scarlett's eye and saw in her face the same simple joy of singing that he was feeling, despite the circumstances.

In the silence that followed, all Gabe could hear was Merry shifting from foot to foot. Gwyn, of course, was totally still.

"Well," said Yates, at last. "Lucien always did know a fine musician when he heard one, but –"

"So did Aurora from what I heard," the flame-haired soldier interrupted with a snigger, and Gabe was surprised by the surge of anger that flooded through him. He'd never wanted to hit anyone in his life, but now it was only Merry's hand on his arm that stopped him stepping forward and punching the man's face.

"That's enough, Dore!" said Yates, and the man stopped smirking. Gabe felt Eddie also stand down.

"Look, you sound better than that last lot," Yates went on, "but if the King is as bad as reports suggest, you won't see him. You might as well pack up and go home."

Gabe's stomach dropped. He had been so sure the plan would work, but it hadn't even gotten them as far as the courtyard.

"Has he not been seen then?" Eddie asked, trying to sound casual, but still earning a suspicious glance from Yates.

"Why'd you want to know?" he asked.

"I, er, well –"

"As true servants of the King, we are all concerned for his welfare," Scarlett said, with a perfect curtsey and a toss of her long blond braid.

"Hmmmph," Yates said, "well, that's as may be, but it's time for you to be off now."

"But —" Eddie protested, stepping forward to plead their case, but Dore snapped his spear upward so that the leaf-shaped blade pointed directly at Eddie's throat.

"Stop!" he snarled. "Not one more step!"

Eddie stepped back, his hands held up to placate the guard as the sound of horses' hooves thundering up the drawbridge was followed immediately by an imperious rapping at the gates.

"Open up, Yates!" came a growl from the other side, and Gabe froze, recognizing Whitmore's harsh tones. Yates's face went white.

"You can't be here!" he hissed at Gabe and the others.

"What'll we do with them?" the tall soldier asked nervously, as Dore wiped frantically at a spot on his armor. "Whitmore'll kill us for letting them in."

"Be quiet!" said Yates, wiping his hands on his pants.

"Just because you were bored," said the tall guard, standing ramrod straight. "Let them in, he said. It'll break up the day, he said."

"Will you *shut up!*" hissed Yates. "How was I supposed to know Whitmore would be back?"

"Er," said Eddie, as the hammering on the door started again and the guards looked at each other in horror. "We could just go on in? Look at us. We're only five minstrels trying to make a living, and if we don't sing for the King, we won't get paid by Lucien."

Merry stepped up beside him. "That's right," she said, sounding woebegone. "Fine working men like yourself wouldn't want us to not get paid, right?"

"Just go!" Yates said, pulling open the smaller door behind him, as Whitmore's voice, now sounding incoherent with rage, came again through the door. "Get out of the way."

Eddie and Merry led the way, and Gabe was barely through the door before Yates shut it behind him. As Gabe followed Gwyn across the inner courtyard, he could hear the gates clanking open behind him and the clatter of hooves and shouting as Whitmore entered. Gabe found himself feeling sorry for Yates and the other guards.

"This way!" said Eddie, taking the lead and hurrying towards the solid stone keep that lay at the heart of the castle. "My father's solar is at the top of the keep."

Merry stopped dead. "We won't be able to just stroll on up there," said Merry. "Not even with your letter."

Eddie also stopped. "Of course," he said, changing direction. "I wasn't thinking. We'll go in through the Great Hall."

He turned towards a long, tall building that clung to the right of the keep, and Gabe was happy to note that it was at least away from the gates, through which Whitmore was now riding, followed by eight dirty, tired-looking men. Gabe wondered how Whitmore would feel if he knew that it was his very arrival that had gotten Eddie back into the castle.

But Merry didn't follow Eddie. "Gwyn," she said, instead. "Where would you go now?"

"Kitchen," said Gwyn, without hesitating. "Singing or no singing, the kitchen's where we'll find out what's what."

"Are you saying that I don't even know my own home?" Eddie said, coming back to them, his face red.

"I'm saying," said Gwyn, one eyebrow raised, "that you know your home as a Prince, but not as a minstrel. Minstrels are servants, not visiting royalty. And servants, no matter how nicely they sing, don't stroll into the solar or the Great Hall. They start at the kitchen."

Merry nodded. "Gwyn's right. We'll go to the kitchen, make ourselves known."

She turned to Eddie. "You do know where the kitchens are, don't you?"

He snorted. "Of course I do," he said, before striding off to the left of the keep, with Scarlett and Midge at his heels. Gabe began to follow, but not before he noticed Merry having a short, whispered conversation with Gwyn, who then attached herself to a group of passing stable boys, her mask suddenly nowhere to be seen. Gabe watched over his shoulder as she passed the smithy's workshop, a sudden flare of heat turning her pale hair orange, before she disappeared like smoke in the direction of the keep.

"Where's she going?" he asked Merry, who caught up to him just as they reached the kitchen door.

"Wherever she likes," said Merry with a wink.

❖

The sun was sinking low over the jagged roof of the prison tower before Gabe and the others finally found themselves standing outside the King's solar. Several times through the long and trying day, Eddie had wanted to unmask himself, pull out his letter from Lucien and demand an audience with his father, but Merry had forestalled him.

"They have no reason to believe that letter is even real," she'd said. "You take off that mask and pull it out now and we'll all be out in the street or worse. Remember, Whitmore is in the castle and we don't know who we can trust and who we can't. It needs to be given directly to the King and you know that."

"My father, you mean," Eddie had said, with a pointed look.

"Your father," she'd replied, patting his hand.

And so they'd talked their way up through the castle, starting with the scullery maids and the kitchen hands, and wending their way through a dizzying array of servants, all of whom seemed to have one purpose and one purpose only – to keep anyone from seeing the King.

Gabe's voice was almost hoarse from having to "show his wares" to every second person they'd met, and even

Scarlett, who loved to perform, was looking flat and tired. Their progress had been made more difficult by the fact that Whitmore's arrival at the castle seemed to have thrown the entire place into disarray, as he stormed about, demanding this and that, the pack of rough-looking soldiers at his back wherever he went.

Of Gwyn, they'd seen no sign.

"Right," said Eddie. "Are we ready? Everyone knows what to do?"

Eddie had warned them that the King was never truly alone. Even in his bed, a place where a person could usually find a quiet moment, he was surrounded by a crowd of servants and counselors, many of whom even Eddie didn't know. Midge had giggled as Eddie had explained the roles of the bed warmer, the cupbearer and, most hilariously for everyone except Eddie, the groom of the stool, whose job it was to empty the King's chamber pot, amongst other things.

"So, er, do you have one of those?" Merry had asked Eddie, struggling to maintain a straight face.

"No!" said Eddie, blushing. "It's only for the King."

There was a short silence. "So you will have one of those one day?" Merry asked, an innocent expression on her face.

"If I ever get my crown back I will," Eddie responded, fiercely.

Gabe had stared at him, trying to imagine the boy who'd slept on the hard ground, endured days and nights in the cold, wind and rain without complaint, and cheerfully mucked in with chores along the way in his other role, his rightful role, as a pampered Prince.

"I might even ask Gabe to do it," said Eddie. "You only ask your most trusted servants for those personal roles."

Gabe blanched. "I'm, er, promised to the Abbey," he said. "But thanks anyway."

Merry looked at him curiously. "Even after all this, you'd still go back there, behind the walls forever?" she asked.

"Well, I . . ." Gabe stammered. The truth was that he was so confused about everything right now that, on one hand, the idea of disappearing back into the serene, safe life at Oldham Abbey looked like a dream. But he couldn't truthfully say that his mind was made up, and that the life of a monk was for him. The betrayal by Prior Dismas and his supporters at the Abbey had rocked Gabe's trust and faith. He'd truly believed that everyone within the walls was a good man, as good as you could get on earth, but now he knew that wasn't the case.

Merry seemed to sense his turmoil. "None of us needs to decide anything about anything at this moment," she said. "We'll concentrate on right now and then we'll take it one step at a time."

Gabe had nodded gratefully.

Now, pushing his tumultuous thoughts aside, Gabe glanced up and down the empty corridor before knocking on the ornate door to the King's solar.

Almost immediately the door opened silently and a pale, thin man dressed in shiny purple pantaloons and matching tunic looked down at them. "Ye-e-es?"

"We're minstrels sent by Lucien, for the King," said Gabe, trying to sound confident. Behind him, Eddie kept his head down.

"I know of no such arrangement," the man said, pushing the door closed.

"Wait!" Before Gabe could act, Merry had stuck her foot in the door, preventing it from shutting. "We've come ever such a long way," she said.

"That," said the man, shoving against the door, "is not my problem."

"Ah, but, you see," said Merry, moving forward, her smile wide and friendly beneath her mask. "It is ours, and Lucien won't be happy if we return without sharing his good wishes."

"Hmmmph," said the man, realizing that she wasn't going to move.

"At least ask the King," said Gabe. "Tell him Lucien sent us. He'll want to see us."

The man stared at Merry. "Kindly remove your foot and I will ask the King what he desires."

"Promise you'll come back?" she said, earning herself a withering glance for her teasing tone.

"Of course," the man said, and shut the door firmly as soon as Merry withdrew her foot.

"This is going well," muttered Eddie.

"It is," said Merry, cheerfully. "You may be used to doors opening for you immediately, but the rest of us have a little more practice at this kind of thing. We're lucky it hasn't taken days to get this far."

Even as she spoke, the door slowly reopened and the man in purple appeared once more. "You can come in," he said. "The King will see you for two minutes, no more."

Entering the gloomy, silent chamber, Gabe's first instinct was to rush over and throw back the heavy velvet drapes to let some light in. A solitary candle flickered by the ornate four-poster bed, throwing dancing shadows against the golden curtains that hung around it. Propped up on a mountain of tapestry pillows lay the King, white-faced and sweating, his unkempt dark hair shot through with gray strands that caught the light.

The man in purple went to stand beside four other servants in the same livery, one holding a glass jug of water, as Gabe and the others shuffled in. At the sight of his father, Eddie let out an involuntary moan, and Gabe felt Midge squeeze in beside him, her hand around his waist.

"Lucien sent you?" the King croaked, sending the servant with the water forward in an instant. The King waved him away. "You saw him?"

"We did, Your Majesty," said Gabe. "He –"

"He is well?" the King asked, cutting Gabe off.

"Very well," said Gabe, wondering whether it was true, even as he said it. For all Gabe knew, Lucien had been tortured by Whitmore and Ronan.

"Hmmph," breathed the King. "Exile agrees with him. Of course it does."

He lapsed into thought momentarily as the hostile servants stared at the intruders. Gabe wondered which of them, if any, were a part of Lord Sherborne's plot. He suspected he would find out when Eddie removed his mask.

"Well, you have a song for me?" the King finally said.

"We do, Your Majesty," said Gabe, gesturing Scarlett forward. He could sense Eddie's impatience, but the plan was that they would sing, to reassure the servants, and then ask for alone time with the King for a special message.

"Wait," said the King, suddenly. "Remove your masks. I want to see Lucien's minstrels for myself. Purvis, another candle if you will."

As the servant who'd opened the door dashed to do the King's bidding, Gabe glanced worriedly at Merry, who shrugged her shoulders helplessly.

"Take them off," she whispered. "We can hardly refuse the King!"

As she began untying her mask, Eddie shrank as far back into the shadows as he could before doing the same.

Scarlett removed her mask and stepped forward into the circle of light created by the candles, her blond hair glowing. But as Gabe did the same and followed her, the King suddenly gasped.

"You!" he spluttered, pointing at them all. "You . . ." He got no further, instead gasping out loud and clutching his chest. Moments later, eyes rolling back in his head, he collapsed against the pillows.

"Father!" Eddie shouted, rushing towards the bed, pushing Gabe out of the way. His exclamation was lost in the tumult around the bed, but his action was not, and two of the servants leapt forward, grabbing Eddie by the arms and wrestling him out of the room.

"Get out!" shrieked Purvis, dabbing at the King's waxy face with a damp cloth. "Get out of here now! What have you done?"

Merry took Gabe's elbow. "Come on!" she shouted. "We have to go!"

"But –" Gabe looked around him with horror, as Midge took his hand.

"No buts," said Merry, pulling on his arm. "Now!"

"Well, well, well," came a booming voice from the doorway. "There I was searching up and down the kingdom for you, and you've saved me all the trouble and come to me."

Merry gasped as Gabe's mouth went dry. "Don't be shy," Whitmore went on, stepping into the solar, seeming to fill the room. "I'm *so very pleased* to see you."

"As," came another voice, as dry as aged timber, "am I."

Gabe felt all the air go out of his body as Ronan of Feldham followed Whitmore into the solar, a struggling Eddie in his grasp. "One for you," said Ronan, patting Eddie on the head, "and one for me." His hard brown stare was directed at Gabe.

"Let me go!" shouted Eddie. "I am Prince Edward and you have no right to have your hands on me. I have a letter to prove it! Purvis! Look at me!"

But Purvis kept his eyes on the floor as Whitmore loomed over him, and Gabe could see the servant shaking even from where he stood. There would be no help for Eddie in this room – everyone in the castle was too scared of Whitmore.

"Ha! Thank you for that," said Whitmore, taking the letter from Eddie's hand as Ronan clamped a hand over the Prince's mouth to silence him. Glancing over at the bed where the King still lay as though asleep, Whitmore smiled.

"I denounce you as an imposter!" he declared, staring coldly at Eddie, as he tore Lucien's letter in four pieces.

He turned to Purvis and the other servants. "The real Prince remains at Rothwell Castle under the protection of our good friend Lord Sherborne," he said, smoothly. "I have been in pursuit of this fake for many weeks now."

The servants all nodded uncertainly, their fear of Whitmore palpable.

"And now we shall remove these scoundrels and allow you to care for the King," Whitmore went on, pushing Ronan, still struggling with Eddie, and the others towards the door and closing it behind them. As it shut, Gabe caught a glimpse of the servants, who had immediately shifted their focus back to the prone figure on the bed, all thoughts of the minstrels forgotten in their concern.

Outside, the hall was eerily silent, as though every resident of the castle had made themselves scarce. Merry looked wildly around and Gabe could see her working out which way to run – but Whitmore grabbed her arm.

"Don't!" he said. "My men await at either end of this corridor and they are on orders to kill anyone who tries to flee."

Merry snatched her arm back, eyes flashing with anger, but she put an arm around a trembling Scarlett and stood quietly.

Whitmore clapped his hands together, a wintry smile of menace on his face. "We meet again," he said to Eddie.

"You won't get away with this!" Eddie spluttered, and Whitmore laughed as Ronan once again gagged Eddie with his calloused hand.

"Oh yes I will," Whitmore smirked. "Particularly when it becomes known that you and your friends murdered the King!"

Eddie froze at the word, while Ronan looked at Whitmore closely.

"Murdered?" he enquired, his hard face deadpan.

Whitmore laughed. "You saw the King!" he said. "He has been dying slowly for more than a year now, even if he doesn't know it. But soon, very soon now, it will be done and who will question me when I point the finger at him?" He sneered at Eddie. "Even better," Whitmore went on, "once we hang him, there will be no question whatsoever to our Prince's claim to the throne."

"Indeed," said Ronan, face impassive, as though discussing the weather. "And what do we do with the rest of them?"

"Whatever we want!" Whitmore said, with a malicious snigger. "Whatever we want. Guards!"

At Whitmore's shout, the eight men that Gabe had seen earlier that day streamed towards them from either end of the hall. Midge slid behind Gabe, trying to hide, and he patted her shoulder, as much to reassure himself as her.

"Take them to the prison tower!" Whitmore almost sang.

Ronan cleared his throat. "There is the small matter of the book," he said, and his tone brooked no argument.

"Ah, yes, the book," said Whitmore, who might be all bluster and menace, Gabe realized, but who seemed to recognize that the ice-cold cruelty at the core of Ronan of Feldham was not to be messed with.

"Eeni, meeni, miney, mo," said Ronan, to Gabe, Merry, Eddie and Scarlett in turn.

"You!" he said, at last, gesturing to Midge. "Don't be shy. Come here."

Midge stepped out from behind Gabe, but not before he could feel her shaking. Straightening her shoulders, she walked towards Ronan.

He reached out and grabbed her by the throat. "Now," Ronan said, tightening his grip and making Midge groan. "Who's got the book?"

Gabe's heart sank. As the keeper of the book he was bound by promise and expectation to keep it safe *at all costs*, but Midge, his friend, was already gasping for breath, her face going red as Ronan's hand squeezed the life out of her.

"I do," he said quietly, putting all his faith in the ancient code in which the book was written. Surely the likes of Ronan and Sherborne would never break it.

But Merry groaned as he spoke. "No, you don't," she reminded him.

Ronan looked from one to the other. "Well, do you or don't you?" he asked, squeezing Midge's frail neck a little harder.

"He doesn't!" Midge wheezed, as though Gabe's admission had given her permission to speak. "I've got it."

"Let her go and she'll show you!" Merry demanded, making Ronan laugh, a strange, wheezing sound.

"She'll show me anyway!" he said, but he let go of Midge, who clutched her throat with both hands, drawing in huge breaths.

"I'm so sorry, Gabe," she wailed, before untying the drawstring bag tied to her waist and unwrapping the book.

"Ah," breathed Ronan, snatching it from her. "The Ateban Cipher."

Gabe blinked back tears as Ronan tucked it casually into his thick leather belt.

"You take it to that Prior of yours," said Whitmore. "Tell him he has one month to unlock its secrets or my soldiers will be paying Oldham Abbey a long and thorough visit. My patience with Sherborne and his hollow promises wears thin."

Now Gabe gulped, thinking of the damage and destruction that Whitmore's men would wreak within the Abbey's peaceful walls.

"Actually," said Whitmore, "take this lot with you as well. We might as well make the Winterfest hangings a gala event."

Gabe froze in horror, barely able to breathe, as Merry stiffened beside him.

163

"Seize them!" Whitmore ordered the soldiers. Gabe felt rough hands grab his arms, and his hands were swiftly tied behind his back. Merry struggled but was quickly subdued with a blow to the side of her head, and Scarlett shrieked as she was grabbed by the hair.

"The morning's soon enough to leave," said Ronan, unmoved by their shouts and struggles. "I could use an ale."

"Yes," agreed Whitmore, slapping the impassive sheriff on the back. "We have much to celebrate." He banged on the door to the King's solar, and Purvis opened it, his head bowed meekly. Gabe wondered if the man had heard anything of what was said out in the hall – but quickly realized that even if he had, nobody would believe him.

"Tell the kitchen to prepare a feast!" Whitmore was saying.

"But the King –" Purvis protested, before Whitmore pulled him out into the hallway.

"A feast," Whitmore repeated, pushing Purvis towards the stairs at the end of the hall. "We will drink to the health of the King."

As Purvis stalked away to do his bidding, Whitmore turned back to Ronan. "Or not," he added in a low voice, a roguish smile on his mawkish features.

"Or not," agreed Ronan, with an answering smirk.

"What are we going to do?" wailed Scarlett for the umpteenth time. She leaned back against the grimy wall of the dungeon, her eyes closed as though warding off pain.

"We're going to stop moaning for starters," said Merry. "Come on, Scarlett, you've had your hissy fit, now it's time to think. Your life depends on it."

"Where's Gwyn?" Scarlett moaned. "You said she'd be here."

"She'd be here if she could," Merry said, and Gabe could hear the underlying worry in her voice. "You know she would."

"What if she's just bolted off to Rothwell to save your pa?" said Eddie, pacing back and forth in the tiny cell. "What if she doesn't even know we're here?"

"Gwyn would never leave me," said Merry, arms folded across her chest.

"Not even for her beloved father?" goaded Scarlett, her beautiful face twisted.

"We're kin, which means I'm going to forget you said that," said Merry, anger rippling through every word. "Although if you open your mouth again I swear I will close it for you."

Scarlett snorted, but said nothing.

"Fighting won't get us anywhere," said Midge, sitting on the hard, stone floor, her arms wrapped around her knees, the white skirt that had looked so lovely earlier that afternoon now dirty with grime. Even in the dim light of the cell, lit only by a solitary torch outside the grated window, Gabe could see the dark marks blooming on the pale skin of her throat, and his fists clenched.

"Nothing's going to get us anywhere," said Eddie, slapping one hand against the solid timber door in frustration. "Nobody's ever escaped the prison tower. Ever."

"Well, there's a first time for everything," said Merry, grimly. "I for one do not intend to wait here for Ronan to fetch me in the morning to take part in a gala hanging."

Swallowing hard at the thought, Gabe stepped over to the grated window, intending to get some fresh air. With five of them crowded into the cramped cell, the air felt stale and sullen, as though it too was a prisoner.

Staring out, Gabe realized he was looking at the cobbled stones of the great inner courtyard of the castle. It was quiet at this time of night, but he could hear the clank of pots and pans banging together as the kitchen staff cleaned up after what must have been a long and festive meal. Gabe felt heartsick just thinking about the celebrations and the loss of the book.

The low murmur of voices nearby caught his ear and he turned to see a pair of large, heavy boots stomp past, followed by the light step of a woman in slippers. They stopped abruptly, their feet facing each other, and the woman giggled softly, her skirts rustling around her. Gabe blushed, realizing they were embracing just a few feet from his face.

"Watch it," came a squeaky man's voice. "You'll catch yourself on that torch."

The woman gathered her skirts in closer. "Surely there's somewhere warmer we can go," she complained.

"Whoa ho," said the man. "You bet there is." With that, the pair ran off together towards the Great Hall, leaving Gabe to watch them go, his brow furrowed. Something the man had just said had given him a glimpse of an idea, but he couldn't quite grasp it. He pressed his face to the grate, trying to get a better view of the courtyard.

"What *are* you doing?" asked Merry, coming to stand beside Gabe, whose face was now pressed against the grate.

"I'm just . . ." Gabe pulled himself up onto his toes and poked his nose through a gap in the bars, trying to see sideways down the wall.

"Trying to burn your nose off on that torch?" Merry joked.

"That's it!" Gabe said, letting the bars go and landing on his heels with a thump. "The torch! That's what I was trying to think of."

"Okay," said Merry. "And why?"

"The door," he said, excitement making his words run together. "It's timber."

Merry frowned, hands on hips. "And?"

"It's timber!" he repeated. "And there's a torch just out there!"

Merry's eyebrows flew up. "And?" she prompted.

"If we can grab the torch, we can burn the door down," Gabe said, feeling suddenly uncertain. "Don't you think?"

Merry laughed. "I do think, Gabe," she said. "I just wanted to see where your plan was going!" She patted his arm. "Well done."

"Right," Merry said, turning to the others. "Who's got the longest arms?"

Despite the fact that Eddie was sure it was him, it turned out that Scarlett's arm was the longest – and the thinnest – so she was tasked with getting the torch.

"Try not to burn yourself," Merry counseled her cousin, earning herself a withering glare before Scarlett stretched her arm out through the grate.

"It's no good," she said after a few seconds. "I can't reach it."

"Try harder," said Merry.

"Or let me have a go," said Eddie, impatience etched on his features.

"Your arm is too big," Midge pointed out. "You wouldn't get past your elbow."

"Yes, but I'd break it trying," said Eddie, "which is more than she's doing."

"Oh, put some hose in it," said Scarlett, standing on her tiptoes and pushing her arm through the grate to her armpit. "I'm doing my best."

"Can you do it a bit faster?" Eddie complained. "It will be morning soon."

"It's no good," said Scarlett. "I can just reach the base of the torch with my fingertips, but I can't grasp it enough to bring it back in here."

Merry groaned. "Come on, Scarlett, this is the most important thing you'll ever do."

"Well, I don't see any of you doing any better," said Scarlett, drawing her arm back in with a toss of her hair.

"I know," said Gabe, trying to ignore the bickering. "What if . . . ? Eddie, get down on all fours near the window."

Eddie grimaced but did as he was told. "Now, Scarlett, stand on his back," said Gabe. "With any luck that will give you just about enough extra stretch to get the torch."

"Don't mind if I do," said Scarlett, jumping onto Eddie's outstretched back with glee as he groaned under her weight. "Oh yes, that's it! I can reach it!"

Very carefully, she drew the torch back through the grate before jumping back to the floor triumphantly.

"Hooray!" said Merry very quietly, clapping her cousin on the back. "I knew you could do it."

"Didn't sound that way," harumphed Scarlett.

"Yes, well, sometimes the best way to get someone to do something is to tell them they can't," said Merry, giving Gabe yet another insight into why she took the lead so often. "Now, stand back. I'm not sure how old this door is, but it looks old, which means it's dry. It should go up like kindling."

Remembering the way the ancient oak tree in which the girls had lived until very recently had gone up in flames in an instant, Gabe flattened himself against the wall as Merry held the torch under one corner of the door and then the other. Within seconds, the door was ablaze, a wall of flame, smoke and heat.

"We're going to cook before we can get out!" shouted Eddie.

"Get down and cover your faces," Merry said, crouching to the floor, and Gabe followed her example.

"Will the guards come?" shouted Midge.

"I'm banking on them being too drunk after Whitmore's feast," said Merry. "I heard them clinking bottles earlier."

Smoke filled the tiny cell as the fire popped and crackled, and Gabe buried his face in his shirt, trying to breathe as shallowly as possible.

"I think it's dying down," said Eddie, what felt like hours later, but was probably only a few minutes.

Gabe peeped towards the door tentatively and saw that Eddie was right. The charred remains of the door smoldered in a heap in the blackened stone doorway, leaving a gap large enough to squeeze through.

"Let's go!" said Merry, dashing towards the door and disappearing through it.

"Do we even know where we're going?" asked Scarlett as she gingerly followed her cousin.

"Away from here," said Eddie, grimly.

Stepping through the door, feeling the heat from the stone warm his face, Gabe found himself in the narrow walkway that wound its way through the dungeons.

"Which way?" Merry asked when they were all in the walkway.

"We can't go right," said Eddie. "It goes to the torture chamber. There's no escape from there. We'll have to go past the guards."

Merry nodded.

"From there, the only way out is across the courtyard," Eddie continued, shaking his head. "Which is one reason no one's ever escaped this tower. It's impossible not to be seen."

"We have no choice," said Merry, giving his shoulder a shake. "It's this way or death, Eddie. If you remember that, you might be amazed at what you can pull off."

With her words ringing in his mind, and very aware of the bright colors of his minstrel costume, Gabe could do nothing but follow where she led. Straight up to the guards' room.

CHAPTER NINE

"Ready?" Merry whispered. Gabe glanced around the guards' room, which seemed filled to the brim with snoring men, and nodded.

"One at a time," Merry said. "Midge, you go first."

Midge didn't hesitate, tiptoeing across the room, picking her way around the sleeping bodies that littered the floor, her slight figure barely seeming to move the air as she went. Gabe held his breath as she reached the last soldier, who was lying across the doorway that led to the vestibule, beyond which the door to the outside lay. The soldiers had clearly been enjoying their festivities too much to remember to close the internal door and create the weather lock that would keep out the winter chill – a fact for which Gabe was eternally grateful. If that soldier had been lying across a closed door, their escape would be impossible.

As it was, Midge leapt gracefully over the sleeping soldier, landing lightly in the vestibule, where she flattened herself against a wall and waited. Merry had decreed that the outside door not be opened until they were all there, ready to run, knowing that the blast of cold air would wake even the drunkest soldier.

Gabe watched anxiously as first Scarlett and then Eddie followed Midge. Eddie landed in the vestibule with a bang, and Gabe held his breath as the soldier in the doorway snorted, rolling over, before settling back into sleep.

"Your turn," whispered Merry, as soon as the soldier was quiet. "Try not to crash about like the King's stag if you can possibly help it."

Suppressing a grin, Gabe began the terrifying journey across the room, aware that the slightest mistake might kill them all. Drawing on years of practice at Oldham Abbey, he willed himself to walk slowly and serenely, as though in meditation or prayer. A sudden image of Prior Dismas's face, telling him off for being distracted yet again, made him stumble and he winced, realizing he'd very nearly stood on a soldier's hand!

Steeling himself, he resolved to show Prior Dismas exactly how focused he could be and began moving again, treading as lightly as he could until, step by achingly slow step, he reached the doorway.

Just one more hurdle, he thought, as Midge, Scarlett and Eddie willed him on with their eyes. For the first time that day, he was glad he was wearing his hose and not the long comforting robes of the Abbey he'd been missing. Trying to jump over a soldier in a long robe would be almost impossible.

Clutching the lute high, Gabe jumped, his heart in his mouth – and landed in the vestibule just as the outside door cracked open, unleashing a cold finger of icy air that whistled through the room like a virago.

Behind him, Gabe felt the room begin to stir as the sleeping soldiers protested against the freezing intrusion. "Get out!" hissed Merry, and Gabe realized she was leaping a path through the men, any thoughts of stealth abandoned.

But Gabe was frozen with horror as the door continued to creak open. He could hear someone muttering to themselves outside.

"Use the lute!" Merry grated. "Pull the door open and smack whoever that is over the head."

Startled, Gabe did as he was told, almost without thought, rushing to the door and pulling it open. The man outside stumbled as the door he'd been leaning on suddenly disappeared. He looked up, and Gabe could see that he'd been sick all over the doorstep, which explained the muttering and the slow way in which the door had opened.

"Hit him!" Merry ordered, and Gabe raised the lute.

"Sorry," he said to the man, before bringing the lute down on his head, trying not to damage either man or instrument too much.

The man fell sideways, dazed. "Run!" Eddie shouted, and Gabe, suddenly aware of the babble of angry voices behind him as the soldiers awoke, jumped over the doorstep, landed in the cobbled courtyard and began running, looking for cover.

"Oi!" came a shout from near the blacksmith's workshop. "Sandals!"

Gwyn! Switching direction, Gabe ran towards the huge stone horse trough that sat to one side of the workshop. It doubled, he knew, as a watering station for the blacksmith's four-legged clients, and as a pool in which to cool the hot iron shoes that he made for them.

"I was just on my way to rescue you," said Gwyn, as he slid behind the trough next to her. "Nice of you to save me the trouble."

"My pleasure," Gabe said, panting, as Midge, Scarlett and Eddie scrambled in beside him.

"Where's Merry?" Gwyn asked, eyes narrowed.

"Isn't she –" Gabe looked around before poking his head above the top of the trough to scan the courtyard.

"She's not there," he said, in despair. "She didn't make it."

Gwyn's eyes narrowed. "You left her behind," she said, staring at them all.

"I thought she was behind me," Eddie said. "She was *right behind me.*"

Gwyn rolled her eyes. "Stay here and look after these," she ordered, dropping a cloth-wrapped package in Gabe's lap before sliding out from behind the horse trough.

"Can we help?" Gabe asked her retreating back, putting the bulky bundle down on the cobbles beside him.

Gwyn turned. "I think you've done enough already, don't you?" she said, in a voice as cold as the winter's night.

With that, she was gone, leaving them to wait, shivering in the dark.

"What's she doing?" asked Eddie, a few moments later as Gwyn crossed the courtyard, marching up to the front door of the prison tower. She hesitated a moment, before ostentatiously stepping over the puddle at the doorstep, and disappearing inside.

"She's going in," Scarlett said, disbelief making her voice sharp. For a moment all was quiet, and then Gabe heard shouts and curses. He prayed that Gwyn was somehow working her faerie magic, taking on a roomful of soldiers and winning.

Minutes later, however, a disheveled guard stood framed in the doorway, staring around with a sneer on his face. He stepped back as four other soldiers fell out into the courtyard.

"Right, split up!" shouted one man, brandishing a short sword. "They have to be here somewhere."

Gabe shrank down behind the trough as the men took off in different directions, fortunately, for now, away from where they were hiding. But for how long? His heart sank even further as he heard a bang and then a click and recognized it as the outer door to the prison tower closing – and being locked from the inside.

Gabe stared at Eddie, Scarlett and Midge, realizing that his own feelings were reflected in their horrified faces.

"What do we do now?" whispered Scarlett.

"We rescue them, of course," Eddie said, stoutly.

Gabe and Midge nodded.

"But how?" Midge asked, echoing Gabe's thoughts.

"I . . . don't know," Eddie admitted. "But we need to think of something – and fast. The sun will be up soon and Ronan will take them to Rothwell."

"He won't go without you, surely?" Gabe asked. "Whitmore was very keen you be hanged there."

Eddie paused. "Ronan doesn't care about me – you saw him in the castle. He only cares about the book. Without that letter that Whitmore tore up, I can't prove who I am anyway." Gabe didn't need to see Eddie's face to know how dejected he felt.

"You can get another letter," Gabe said, trying to make him feel better.

"It will be too late to save Ralf Hodges," Eddie said. "Too late to save Merry and Gwyn. Too late for –"

He broke off, and Gabe could hear him swallow hard before he continued. "Too late, perhaps, for my father," Eddie continued in a whisper. "Who knows what's happening to him while I hide in the dark like a child."

Gabe stared at the cold, hard stones under his knees. At Oldham Abbey, he'd been taught to pray in times of crisis, to ask for help and to put his faith in God to deliver that help. And part of him wanted to do just that, right now – but that part of him felt like a different Gabe.

"Gwyn and Merry wouldn't just sit here wondering," he said, out loud. "They would *do* something."

Being around the girls had shown him that prayer was not enough. If someone was starving, like Widow Goodman had been, it wasn't enough to expect God to deliver – instead, it was important to offer a helping hand. Gabe didn't always agree with the method the girls employed in their assistance, but he couldn't argue with the results. They always acted out of kindness, love and charity – but they always acted.

"We're not going to be able to break them out of the tower," Gabe said, thinking fast. "The best thing we can do is to get out of here ourselves, get the horse and cart and get to Rothwell as soon as we can."

"What?" hissed Scarlett, while Midge gasped. "No! We can't leave them behind."

"Gabe's right," said Eddie. "If we stay here, we'll all get caught. We know where they're headed and we can come up with a plan to rescue the girls before they get there."

"And just who's going to come up with this plan?" demanded Scarlett. "Merry and Gwyn are both in *there*."

"We'll have to do it," said Gabe, his mouth dry. "They've both rescued us, all of us, at some stage and now it's up to us to return the favor."

"But what if we can't?" wailed Midge.

Eddie put a hand on her shoulder. "We just have to," he said, simply. "We don't have a choice. Merry and Gwyn are relying on the four of us and so we're just going to have to work it out."

"So, what do you say?" asked Gabe, needing their support.

Midge nodded, her eyes shining with tears. Scarlett hesitated, biting her lip, before she too agreed.

"Right," said Gabe, bundling up the package that Gwyn had left with him. "The first step is to get ourselves out of here without being caught."

He rose cautiously on his knees until his eyes were just above the line of the trough. A group of soldiers was over near the gatehouse, listening as one man waved his arms around. Other than that, there was no movement in the courtyard.

"Eddie," Gabe said, sinking back down. "Is there any way out of the castle other than the front gates?"

Eddie frowned. "There's a postern behind the keep," he said. "But it's always locked."

"What's a postern?" Midge asked.

"A tiny gate set deep into the walls," Eddie said. "It's been there since the castle was built by my grandfather, but no one ever uses it."

"Could you get it open?" asked Gabe.

"I . . . don't know," Eddie said, pursing his lips. "There's a key, somewhere. Perhaps in the larder?"

"The larder?" Gabe said, startled.

Eddie grinned. "All the spare keys are stashed in the larder, in a wooden box behind the preserves. Only the family and the head cook know about them."

"Seriously?" said Scarlett. "The royal family keeps its keys in the larder? What kind of security is that?"

"Where does your father keep yours?" Eddie asked.

"In a secret strongbox," said Scarlett, sounding bored. "The key to which he keeps around his neck."

Eddie laughed. "And if I were a serious thief, that's the first place I would look," he said. "Nobody ever thinks to search the larder."

There was a pause while they all considered this.

"Well, it makes our job easier," Gabe said. "We just need to get to the larder and find the right key."

But Eddie was shaking his head. "Cook guards that kitchen more fiercely than any soldier," he said. "You saw her. She wouldn't even let us in the door – just sent us to the butler. I've heard she even gets up early so she can be first in there. She'll be there now."

Scarlett looked shocked. "But surely that's a scullery maid's job?"

"You would think so," said Eddie. "But nobody argues with her. She's the best cook in the kingdom and she does things her way."

"Well, what are we going to do then?" asked Scarlett. "How can we get to the key?"

Gabe considered. "We need to send someone she'd never be suspicious of," he said, turning to Midge. "Do you think you could distract her?"

Midge nodded. "I can try."

"Okay, then, while you do that . . ." Gabe paused.

"Yes?" Scarlett prompted.

"While you do that, I'll slip into the larder and take the box of keys," Gabe finished, wishing it could be one of the others. "Scarlett and Eddie are both too big and I'm used to walking quietly and being still when I need to be."

He'd watched Gwyn in action enough times to know that these were two of the most important skills when it came to going places you weren't supposed to be.

"Well, if you're sure," said Eddie, looking uncertain.

"I am," said Gabe, trying to sound more confident than he felt. He raised himself back up above the trough, shuddering when he saw that the group of soldiers around the gatehouse had doubled in size and that more were heading to join them. An organized search was not far away.

"Let's go," he said to Midge, handing Gwyn's bundle to Scarlett. "Look after this. We don't have much time."

"Wait," Eddie said, slipping off his white shirt. "At least take this shirt. You're very . . . obvious in that blue one."

Gabe nodded, slipping off his own shirt and replacing it with Eddie's, which hung longer than his own and covered more of his red hose. His last sight as he ducked around the horse trough and began to follow Midge towards the kitchen door, sticking to the shadows cast by the huge castle walls, was of Eddie struggling into the blue shirt, which was at least two sizes too small for him.

Midge paused near the kitchen door, and Gabe caught up with her. "Knock and tell her you're hungry," he said. "Try to get her talking and move away from the door. I'll get in and out as quick as I can."

He stepped away and ducked around the corner, flattening himself against the wall and keeping a wary eye on the soldiers, who were now fanning across the courtyard, skewering the haystack by the stables with their swords and spears and looking into water barrels. Fortunately, they'd started in the corner away from the prison tower and the smithy's shop, so Eddie and Scarlett were okay for now.

He heard Midge's soft knock on the kitchen door, followed by a quick tread and some muttering from inside the kitchen.

"What do you want?" came a sharp, woman's voice. Gabe knew from their visit to the kitchen the day before that the head cook was a short, gray-haired, harried woman, whose face seemed permanently red from the heat of her stove.

Gabe heard Midge's murmured response, and imagined her staring up at the woman with those big, brown eyes. In her thin skirt and blouse, dark shadows under her eyes from tiredness, and her face pinched with worry about Gwyn and Merry, she would be hard to ignore.

"There, there, love," said the cook. "You come right on in here and I'll get you a bowl of lovely warm porridge. You look all done in."

The kitchen door opened wide enough for the light inside to spill out onto the courtyard, and Gabe counted to three before ducking around the corner. He let out a sigh of relief when he saw that the door had been left open, whether by mistake or because Midge had done it.

Gabe sidled to the door and popped his head inside, checking quickly that the coast was clear. Midge had followed the cook over to the big hearth where a huge pot hung over smoldering embers. She'd been clever enough to stand to the left of the cook, chatting away to her in a high piping voice, keeping the woman's attention fixed away from the open larder door.

In a trice, Gabe had scampered across the kitchen floor, the flagstones absorbing his light step, and was inside the larder, breathing hard, his heart pounding.

Trying to calm his thoughts, Gabe took stock of his surroundings, shivering in Eddie's thin shirt. The white-washed stone walls of the larder were designed to keep the small room dark and cool and they were definitely doing their job. Deep shelves lined the walls, reaching up high over his head, with barrels and boxes stacked beneath them. Gabe looked up at the ceiling, noticing three pheasants hanging by their feet, ready for plucking.

Feeling slightly ill, Gabe forced himself to concentrate. Eddie had said the key box was behind the preserves. Turning to his right, he came face-to-face with a long shelf laden with tall jars of golden peaches, plump yellow pears and purple plums. Ignoring the rumbling of his tummy, he cautiously removed a jar of peaches and stuck his arm in behind, feeling about gently. Nothing.

Replacing the peaches, he moved along the shelf, discovering pickled onions, carrots sliced into tiny moons and wheels of cheese stacked four-high. Taking down a jar of onions, he felt behind the vegetables. He was beginning to panic when his fingers finally caught the corner of a wooden box, pushed way back and covered, judging by the stickiness on his hand, in cobwebs. Relief surged through him, and Gabe gingerly dragged the box forward, one ear on the conversation in the kitchen.

The box was small and deep, but heavy. Made from rosewood, its corners were picked out in maple, and it featured a golden clasp in the shape of a horseshoe. Gabe quickly flicked the clasp open, smiling when he discovered six keys nestled snugly inside. Not knowing which one he needed, and hoping that Eddie did, he closed the box and crept to the larder door.

"Oh no," Midge was saying. "My ma and pa take good care of me, but they're sleeping with the other travelers in the Great Hall."

Poking his head around the door, Gabe caught her eye and nodded in the direction of the courtyard. Midge didn't so much as blink in his direction, continuing to chat away to the concerned cook about her doting parents as Gabe stole across the flagstones.

Approaching the door, Gabe couldn't stop himself from rushing – which was probably how he missed the tiny gap in the flagstones, catching the toe of his boot in it. Stumbling forward, he clutched the keys convulsively, aware that the slightest jangle would give him away. Stopping himself just before he hit the door jamb, Gabe risked a quick look back over his shoulder. Midge had maneuvered herself so that the cook's back was to the door, but Gabe could see that Midge was trying very hard not to look at him. It was definitely time to go.

With a quick look left and right to make sure there weren't any soldiers lying in wait, he stepped out through the kitchen door and ducked around the corner. It was only when he exhaled, long and slow, that Gabe recognized he'd been holding his breath since he'd set foot outside the larder.

Inside, he heard Midge's voice thanking the cook and making her goodbyes, before she skedaddled out the door and around the corner next to him, her eyes dancing.

"Well done," Gabe whispered.

"And to you," she said. "But I think we'd best get going."

One by one they darted across the courtyard to the horse trough, which was looking more exposed now that the first rays of morning light were sliding over the castle walls.

"Did you get it?" Eddie whispered, as Gabe slid in beside him.

Gabe handed him the heavy box and Eddie immediately opened it.

"Do you know which one it is?" Scarlett asked. "Those soldiers are getting closer."

"No," said Eddie, frustrated. "I'm going to have to try them all."

"Best we go and do that," said Gabe, with a frown. "Lead the way, Eddie."

Sticking the box in his pocket, Eddie nodded, before scrambling away, leading them around the back of the blacksmith's forge. Squeezing between the castle wall and the tall stone chimney that marked the back of the forge, Gabe could feel the residual heat on his face. He wanted nothing more than to lean against the chimney and warm himself through, but there was no time to waste.

Ducking and weaving, Eddie led them on a meandering path around the keep, arriving at last in the narrow corridor between the keep wall and the castle's rear entrance. Here, the sun's rays couldn't penetrate between the two tall walls of stone, and the resulting chill seemed to rise up through Gabe's boots and into his very hair.

Eddie was fumbling before a small, heavy iron gate, not much taller or wider than he was, and set deep into the thick stone walls, with barely a crack around it.

"Most people don't even know this is here," he said, trying first one key and then another. "Nobody ever comes this way – there's no reason to."

"No reason not to hurry up either," said Scarlett, looking anxiously left and right. Gabe could hear the shouts and heavy footsteps of the soldiers in the courtyard, and knew they had not given up their search.

"Hold your horses," said Eddie. "I'm doing my best." As he spoke, there was a ringing sound as a key hit the cobblestones, and Eddie cursed under his breath.

"You'd do better if you didn't drop them," goaded Scarlett.

"And you, of course, would do better full stop," said Eddie, but he bent back to his task, trying the key he'd dropped.

"Gabe," said Midge, "I think someone is coming."

They all froze, listening hard. Sure enough, the sound of footsteps was getting closer.

"How many more do you need to try?" asked Gabe.

"Three," said Eddie.

"Make an educated guess as to which one it might be and try that next," advised Gabe.

Eddie examined the three remaining keys in the box, before reaching in and picking one out.

"Cross your fingers," he said to the others, before putting the key in the lock. Gabe held his breath, time seeming to slow as Eddie turned the key and the footsteps became louder and louder, closer and closer. He glanced over his shoulder – just as a soldier loomed into view around the corner of the keep.

"Oi!" came a loud shout. "They're 'ere! Stop! You!"

"Eddie," moaned Gabe, urgency making his voice crack.

"I've got it!" Eddie said triumphantly as the key turned.

"No time for celebrations," said Scarlett. "Let's go!"

Eddie reefed the gate open, and dashed through it, and the others followed swiftly as the soldier drew closer.

"We have to shut it!" shouted Gabe, pulling the gate behind him. "We have to lock it!"

Eddie stepped forward, key in hand. As Gabe clanged the gate shut, Eddie shoved the key in, just as the soldier reached the other side.

"Oh no you don't!" he yelled, grabbing at the handle, yellow teeth flashing.

"Oh yes we do!" said Scarlett, as she rushed to help Gabe hold the gate shut, Midge joining her. Desperately they all clung to the gate, pulling against it with all their might as the roaring soldier tried to open it from his side.

Just as Gabe thought they were going to lose the battle of strength, he heard a loud click and Eddie held the key aloft, beaming at the soldier.

"Sorry, you'll have to go the long way round," he said with a short bow, before Gabe grabbed him by the arm.

"The sun's up," he said. "They'll be leaving any minute and we still have the horse to collect."

As they ran through the quiet streets around the castle, Callchester was just beginning to stir. Watching as a washerwoman put a saucer of milk on her doorstep before picking up a basket of linens, Gabe was surprised to remember that, to most people, this was just another day.

But, if they didn't manage to get to Rothwell by tomorrow, it could be Merry and Gwyn's last full day on earth.

CHAPTER TEN

They weren't going to make it. Gabe rubbed his weary eyes and pulled his cloak more tightly around him, feeling every movement of the cart on the rocky road. An owl hooted somewhere in the trees, and Delphine flicked her ears in response.

"We only have to be there before noon tomorrow," Scarlett repeated, for the umpteenth time since the sun had gone down on what felt like the longest day of Gabe's life. "The Winterfest hangings are always at noon."

Gabe glanced at Eddie, holding the reins and staring stoically ahead, and knew he was thinking what Gabe was thinking: they needed as much time as possible to have any chance of rescuing the girls.

Midge stroked Albert's feathers as he sat on her lap. "I'm going to release him to get his dinner," she said, standing up on the moving cart and removing Albert's hood.

"Lucky Albert," muttered Eddie, and Gabe's own stomach growled in response. They'd been on the road all day and half the night, and were still a good half day's ride from Rothwell. Gabe had hoped to move much more quickly, but had forgotten about Delphine's sore hoof. They had tried to convince the hosteler to let them have two horses instead, leaving Delphine and the cart for security, but he'd been obstinate, particularly once he'd noticed the lame leg.

"I wish Borlan was here," Midge said now. "We'd be there in a trice."

"Well, he's not," said Gabe, "so we'll have to make do." Just like Gwyn and Merry weren't there, and they were having to make do without them.

"Nicholas will follow," he added.

"Assuming the stable boy passes on the message," Eddie said, staring straight ahead. Gabe glanced at him, worried about Eddie's gloomy frame of mind. The excitement of getting through the back gate and locking it had carried him nearly all the way to the stables.

But it had disappeared in an instant, when they'd been forced to hide near the stables as a huge complement of soldiers had ridden past at full speed, followed by a shuttered carriage, and then by Ronan of Feldham and Whitmore, both grim faced.

"Merry and Gwyn were in that carriage," Scarlett had spluttered, as they'd crawled from their hiding place. "We'll never catch up to them."

"We have to try," said Midge, and the others had nodded, saying nothing for there was nothing to say.

Now Gabe shifted on the hard seat next to Eddie, wishing that he could fly like Albert. As he moved, his foot kicked the bundle that Gwyn had left with him and he reached under the seat to pull it out, intending to put it in the back with Scarlett and Midge.

"What is that anyway?" Eddie asked, sounding interested for the first time since they'd left Callchester. Gabe had let him stew in stony silence for most of the journey, knowing that he was lost in thoughts of his father. For his part, Gabe was swinging between despair about the danger that Merry and Gwyn were in, and hopelessness as he thought of the Ateban Cipher.

"I don't know," Gabe admitted now, staring at Gwyn's bundle. "I don't even know where she got it from." He'd simply carried the bundle because Gwyn had asked him to do so, and then tucked it under the seat in the flurry of movement as they'd left the stables, securing Gwyn's precious teacup beside it to keep it safe.

At least they'd managed to get the teacup back, he thought. Midge had led them to the merchant where Gwyn had left it as security against the minstrel clothes they'd borrowed. The hard-faced trader hadn't wanted to give it to them because Merry and Gwyn's clothes were, of course, missing, but Midge had turned those huge brown eyes on her and managed to convince the woman the others were not far behind them.

He glanced beneath the seat now to make sure the teacup was still safe, even as he wondered if they would ever get the chance to show it to Gwyn.

"Open it," said Scarlett now, leaning forward to nudge the bundle. "We might be able to use it somehow. She wouldn't have given it to you if it wasn't important."

Gabe blushed, wondering if he should have been more curious about the package. It was too big to be the Ateban Cipher and so, he had to admit with a pang, he'd lost interest in it. What if Gwyn had intended for him to open it much sooner? What if there was something in it that might have helped them to rescue Gwyn and Merry?

Feeling like an idiot, he placed the bundle on his lap and examined it more closely. It was wrapped, he noticed, in a light, fine cloth in a pale gold color that gleamed in the dying sunlight, secured with a soft cord made of braided purple thread. Gabe frowned – was that silk? And where had he seen that pale gold color before?

Eddie glanced across. "That's my father's pillowcase!" he exclaimed.

Gabe gasped. "Are you sure?"

"Yes," said Eddie, pulling so hard on the reins that Delphine came to a stop. "And that purple cord's the curtain tie from his bed!"

"But Gwyn wasn't in your father's solar," said Gabe.

"Well, that pillowcase says differently," said Eddie, impatiently. "Open it, Gabe!"

With trembling hands, Gabe unwrapped the tidy bundle as Scarlett and Midge pressed behind him, looking over his shoulder. When the folds of fabric fell back, Scarlett let out a gasp.

"It's a painting!" she said. "Unroll it, Gabe."

Gabe did as he was told, and something dropped into his lap.

"It's Hayden's Mont," said Eddie, in awe. "She's cut the painting from the frame in my father's solar."

"It's the Ateban Cipher!" Gabe said, at the same time, hand on the manuscript in his lap. "She got it back!"

The two boys stared at each other.

"How did she do it?" Eddie asked.

"I don't know," replied Gabe, shaking his head in wonder.

"Why did she take the painting?" Scarlett asked. "What good will it do?"

"I don't know," said Eddie, holding the painting by its edges so that he could stare at it. "But she must have had her reasons."

"Maybe it's that," said Midge, pointing to the bottom corner, which had curled in slightly.

"There's something fixed to the back of the painting," said Eddie. "An envelope, sealed with a wolf. Father's seal."

"Open it," said Scarlett. "It must be important."

"There's no point opening it now," said Eddie, sounding frustrated. "It's too dark to read it and we don't have so much as a candle between us. We'll leave it where it's safe and look at it in the morning."

"And in the meantime?" said Scarlett, sounding miffed.

"In the meantime, we keep going," said Eddie, clicking his tongue and giving Delphine the signal to walk on. "Gwyn has risked so much for us that I'll be darned if I'm going to let Lord Sherborne have her."

"He's already got her!" Scarlett wailed. "And he's going to hang her! What can we do about it?"

"I don't know," said Gabe, looking down at the book in his hands. "But we'll think of something. We have to."

❖

The noise of the crowd was overwhelming, packed as they were, shoulder to shoulder, in the great courtyard at Rothwell Castle. Gabe tried to breathe through his mouth, but the stench of unwashed bodies, damp clothing, cabbage and ale assailed his nostrils.

"I'm going to be sick," Scarlett whispered in his ear. She was squeezed against Gabe with Midge tucked in front of her. "This is awful."

"They're so . . . happy," said Eddie, on Gabe's other side. "Look at them. People are going to die here and they're excited about it."

"They're just glad it's not them," said Gabe. "Come on, we need to get out of here. We're not going to be able to do anything from here."

"We're not going to be able to do anything anyway," hissed Scarlett, though she turned and began to weave her way through the press of bodies, guiding Midge before her. Staying close, Gabe put his head down and followed her, using his elbows to create a path, feeling Eddie do the same behind him.

"Did you see the girls?" Eddie asked, as they finally found some space at the back of the crowd. It seemed as though everyone in the shire had made their way to the castle for the Winterfest celebrations, which would kick off with the hangings at noon. Gabe could see the wooden platform, constructed especially for the day, showcasing three nooses blowing back and forth in the wind, swinging from the sturdy gallows.

The crowd expected three hangings – Ralf Hodges and two other men brought up from the dungeon, blinking into the pale, gray light, and corralled now, cold and shivering, in a wooden cage set to one side. But Gabe knew they were going to get five.

"I didn't," he responded. "They must be keeping them out of sight. Maybe we can find them while the crowd is distracted."

"While Lord Sherborne hangs my uncle, you mean?" said Scarlett, with a grimace. "Even if we save Merry and Gwyn then, they'll never forgive us for letting their pa hang."

Gabe exhaled sharply. "I don't know what else to do," he admitted. "It's not like we can go up there in front of all these people and set him free."

"You've got the book," Scarlett reminded him. "Perhaps that's why Gwyn retrieved it. To use it to bargain for her pa's life."

Gabe felt tears spring to his eyes, torn between wanting to help Ralf Hodges and his role as keeper of the book. "I can't," he groaned. "I realized when Ronan had it what a terrible betrayal it was to give it over. I can't do it again. I can't."

"Imagine what they'll do to Uncle Ralf, Merry and Gwyn if you don't!" hissed Scarlett.

"Don't," Midge said, her hand on Scarlett's arm. "Don't do this. If we fight amongst ourselves now, we'll never be able to save them."

Eddie nodded. "She's right," he said, quietly. "We need to come up with a plan."

"Sorry," said Scarlett, and Gabe could see that she was crying. "I know how important the book is, but – they're all I have . . . Merry and Gwyn. Without them, I'd be lost."

Gabe felt for the book, safely tucked into its customary position in the small of his back. It felt like a stone had wedged itself there, heavy and sharp. He could hear Lucien's words in his mind: "Keep it safe. No matter what."

How easy it would be to take it to Sherborne now and demand the release of the prisoners. But where would that leave all of these people around him, then? What would it mean for the future of Alban?

"I'm sorry," he said to Scarlett. "We need to find another way."

"And we need to do it soon," said Midge, pointing at the platform, her voice filled with horror. "Look!"

Gabe turned to see Lord Sherborne mounting the stage, resplendent in robes of shiny red material embossed with gold thread. He was closely followed by the imposter Prince, looking dazed in a purple velvet cloak over white tunic and breeches, and Gabe could hear Eddie hissing through his teeth at the sight.

"Are you all right?" Gabe asked his friend.

"Oh, let's see," said Eddie. "I last saw my father lying unconscious, my friends are about to be hanged, and there's someone up there pretending to be me . . . On the whole, I'd say all right probably doesn't begin to touch the sides."

Gabe swallowed. "I'm sorry," he said. "I only meant –"

"No," said Eddie, suddenly, shaking his head, as Whitmore and Ronan of Feldham strode up the stairs to the platform. "No, *I'm* sorry, Gabe. There's no point in taking it out on you when the real villains are parading about up there."

As Gabe watched Whitmore and Ronan waving to the crowd, looking very pleased with themselves, he felt something inside him twist. It was so unfair that the crowd was cheering them on when they were in the middle of a plot to overthrow the King!

The twist became a knifing pain when Prior Dismas and Damman stepped up and waved to the crowd. This time, however, the response was lukewarm, with an occasional daring "boo" sounding from the throng, which made the pair step back hurriedly to stand behind Whitmore and Ronan.

Wondering about the boos, Gabe scanned the faces around him. Most were full of excited anticipation, but some . . . Gabe recognized Widow Goodman at the edge of the crowd, her children nestled around her. Over there was the tall man who had bought the horse that Merry and Gwyn had "acquired" on the Rothwell Road. The proceeds of that sale had gone to Widow Goodman.

He noticed Scarlett nodding at a young woman standing in a knot of people a few yards to their right. "Who's that?" he asked.

"The Burney family," she said. "Merry helped them out of a tight spot last winter."

Gabe's breathing quickened. "Do you recognize anyone else here?" he asked.

"Yes," she said, and began pointing out faces and groups in the crowd. "That's the Thurtells, the Farrers, the Smiths – oh, and over there is Bert Brown. Merry paid a blacksmith's debt for him last autumn so he could get his horse shod. And there's –"

"Do you think they know that Ralf Hodges is to be hanged today?" Gabe interrupted.

She looked confused. "I shouldn't think so," she said, slowly. "But then I don't know that they'd know who he was. Merry and Gwyn don't go dropping their names about the place. None of us do."

"Oh," breathed Gabe, "that's good."

She frowned. "Why?"

Gabe opened his mouth to explain, but the man in front turned to shush him. "Lord Sherborne's talking," he said. "And while I don't care much for the man, I don't want to be flogged by those soldiers for not listening."

Gabe nodded, turning his attention to the stage.

"And so we come to Winterfest," Lord Sherborne was saying. "A time when we sweep away our mistakes to make way for the spring to come."

The crowd cheered.

"It has been a hard year," Lord Sherborne said, his voice dropping to a sonorous murmur.

The crowd mumbled agreement, shifting restlessly.

"For all of us," Lord Sherborne said, as his glittering thread caught the sun.

"Not for you!" came a shout behind Gabe, followed by the sound of heavy boots. Gabe turned to see a man cowering under the blows of three soldiers.

"For all of us," Lord Sherborne repeated, glaring over the crowd. He paused dramatically. "A hard year demands respite," he said. "You came here today expecting wine, food and hangings."

The crowd cheered.

"And these you shall have!" Lord Sherborne said, waving his arms overhead. "You expect three hangings – murderers, thieves and poachers the lot of them! Men who break the laws of our land and expect to get away with it. Men who think they deserve MORE THAN THE REST OF US. But they shall not have it!"

"Nooooooo!" howled the crowd, pressing forward, carrying Gabe and the others with them.

"They shall have PUNISHMENT!" bellowed Lord Sherborne, clearly enjoying himself now that he felt the crowd was onside.

"Yeesssssss!" roared the crowd, and Gabe could see people around him were dazed and excited. Prior Dismas was rubbing his hands together, his thin lips twisted into a smile.

"We shall have REVENGE!" Lord Sherborne howled. "And we shall have it FIVE TIMES OVER!"

"FIVE!" the crowd shouted, jumping up and down.

"How can they be like this?" asked Midge, her hands over her ears. "Look at them. They're talking about people!"

"Not anymore," said Gabe, grimly. "They're caught up in the bloodlust. We need to get out of this." Picking up Midge, who was now crying with fear, he carried her to a quiet corner of the courtyard. All other eyes were on

Lord Sherborne, who was still prancing along the platform, rousing the crowd into a frenzy.

"What can we do?" asked Scarlett.

"I thought I had an idea," said Gabe, despairing, "but now . . ."

"What was it?" asked Eddie, grabbing his arm.

"The crowd," Gabe said. "There are so many people here that Merry and Gwyn have helped. I thought if the crowd saw them, that it might turn against Lord Sherborne and help us."

Eddie glanced at the restless crowd around them, still hooting and catcalling.

"I can't see it," he said, pointing at the platform. "Particularly when the girls aren't even here – and their pa will be hanged any minute. The executioner is there."

Gabe turned to the stage, his eyes following Eddie's finger. A mountain of a man with a bald head and huge hands was stepping onto the stage, cracking his knuckles. At the sight of him, the crowd went even crazier, while Lord Sherborne beamed.

"It's all we've got!" said Gabe. "But I don't know how to make it work. We need more time."

"We don't have time!" shrieked Scarlett, tears rolling down her face as the executioner proceeded to pull down hard on each of the nooses, testing the strength of the gallows.

"Prepare the prisoners!" Lord Sherborne shouted over the wild baying of the crowd, which sounded like an animal with hundreds of heads. Nothing could distract their attention now.

Except . . .

"Midge," Gabe said, putting his arm around her. "Where's Albert?"

"I was going to leave him with the cart," she said, sounding surprised. "But he was hungry. He'll be in the woods outside the walls."

"Can you call him from here?" he asked, tension making his voice sound high even to his own ears.

"I can try," she said. "It's noisy but . . ."

"What do you want him for?" Eddie asked. "If you bring him in here, one of those archers will just shoot him down."

Gabe swallowed. He hadn't thought of that.

"Bah," said Midge, with a small grin. "He's too fast for them. What do you want him to do?"

"We need a distraction," Gabe said.

Midge simply nodded and, putting two fingers in her mouth, whistled for Albert. Gabe scanned the sky anxiously as the crowd around them pressed in, but there was no sign of the majestic bird.

"He can't hear you," Gabe said, despairing.

"I'll try again," said Midge, whistling. But her whistle was drowned out by a group of farm workers standing nearby, who thought she was showing her support for Lord Sherborne and began whistling as well, a deafening cacophony of tuneless, earsplitting shrieks.

On the platform, Lord Sherborne beamed. "It's time!" he bellowed. "The prisoners shall be hanged in order of worst crimes to least."

The executioner took up his position at the top of the stairs to the platform, waiting to escort the first prisoner. After a beat or two, he peered down the stairs, where a scuffle seemed to be taking place. A hush settled over the crowd as it awaited the first star in the main spectacle of the day.

And into that hush, Midge sent another, desperate whistle for Albert.

Gabe's mouth was dry as he tried to keep one eye on the platform and one on the dull gray sky above him. The crowd was now so quiet that he fancied he could hear a tiny squeak as the nooses swayed in the wind. A soldier cursed.

And then a tiny figure, bound hand and feet and gagged, was carried up onto the platform and Gabe's hopes crashed around his feet.

"Ladies and gentlemen," said Lord Sherborne excitedly to the stunned crowd. "I give you the first of the Rothwell brigands, who've been terrorizing travelers in this shire for nearly two years."

With tears in his eyes, Gabe watched as a soldier unceremoniously dumped Gwyn on her feet behind a noose, where she stood, unblinking, staring defiantly at the crowd.

"That's just a lass!" shouted a deep male voice from the front of the crowd. The farm workers near Gabe shifted position for a better look. The man who'd bought the horse from Gwyn was up on his toes, staring at the stage.

"She may look like 'just a lass,'" said Lord Sherborne in a menacing voice, "but she's a thief and a guttersnipe and a traitor."

The crowd shifted restlessly and Whitmore stepped forward. "In the name of the King, I declare Gwynfor Hodges a traitor," he said, smoothly. "Stealing from the common people for profit."

"That's not true!" shouted Scarlett. "She never stole from anyone who couldn't afford it."

But her voice was drowned out in the boos and hisses from the crowd.

Gwyn simply stared out over the crowd, her face a mask behind the gag.

"And," Whitmore went on, throwing out an arm in the direction of the stairs and forcing Lord Sherborne to take a step back, "I lay the same charges on Merryn Hodges, and sentence them both to hang."

But the sight of Merry's red hair as she was dragged up onto the platform to stand behind the noose next to Gwyn's had the crowd buzzing again. Gabe glanced over at Widow Goodman who was frowning and whispering to the woman standing beside her.

"Midge," Gabe said in a low voice. "Go through the crowd, find anyone you can that the girls have helped. *Tell them* who they are. *Tell them.*"

"What about me?" Scarlett said. "I know some of them, too."

Gabe nodded. "Be quick!"

"You don't have enough time to start a riot!" said Eddie.

"I have enough time to try," said Gabe.

"We'll be killed," Eddie warned. "If they catch us, we're dead."

"If we don't, Merry and Gwyn are dead," Gabe said before raising his voice.

"Lies!" he shouted. "Lies!"

The farm workers beside him looked at him with interest. "Lies!" they shouted, taking up the cry despite not knowing what Gabe was talking about.

Ducking behind them, grabbing Eddie by the arm, Gabe began making his way to the edge of the crowd, keeping his eyes on Whitmore, who was scanning their section of the crowd, his face angry. As Gabe watched, Whitmore nodded at three soldiers who began fighting their way through the heaving crowd, forcing a path to where the farm workers were still shouting.

Even as Gabe watched, he saw other pockets of the crowd take up the call, the message spreading as Midge and Scarlett moved through it.

The smile on Lord Sherborne's face began to slip, and Gabe saw Prior Dismas glance nervously around him.

"Hang them!" Whitmore screamed, and the executioner stepped towards the nooses.

"Noooo!" shouted Gabe, trying to push his way forward, not knowing what he thought he was going to do, but desperate to do *something* to help his friends.

But now the mood of the crowd was changing, and the cry of "Lies" was taken up by more and more voices. All around Gabe, angry men and women were waving their arms, their faces red and contorted, pressing forward towards the platform where the executioner was now standing in front of the girls, theatrically opening a trapdoor before each of their feet. Neither Merry nor Gwyn moved.

"We have to get out of here!" Eddie said, pulling on the back of Gabe's tunic, staring up at the battlements where Lord Sherborne's archers were drawing up their bows, awaiting a signal to fire upon the restless crowd.

Whitmore was bellowing at the executioner to get on with it, and the huge man shot him a weary look before stepping around the girls, preparing to place the nooses over their thin necks.

Ronan of Feldham stood like stone, keeping a wary eye on the writhing crowd, but Lord Sherborne, Gabe noticed, was sidling in the direction of the stairs. And all the time, the fake Prince sat on his throne, staring vacantly ahead.

Then Albert appeared, rising over the top of the castle wall, pausing majestically before swooping into the courtyard, his raucous screeching causing all but the bravest of men to throw themselves to the cobblestones. He blasted upward, towards the sky, lazily looping around, and Gabe frantically searched the crowd for Midge.

With a pang of terror, he saw her. She'd wormed her way to the front of the crowd and was standing on the ground right beside the gallows. Gabe stood openmouthed as she calmly put her fingers in her mouth and whistled. He wasn't close enough to hear her command over the roar of the crowd, but the effect on Albert was immediate. He turned almost on the spot and swooped, on a course that took him right through the middle of the group standing on the platform.

Eddie grabbed Gabe's arm. "What's she doing?"

"I don't know," said Gabe, unable to take his eyes off the scene unfolding as the magnificent bird shot like an arrow through the group, twisting and turning so fast it was almost impossible to make out his movements as he hurtled into the tiny gap between the executioner and the two girls.

In fright, the executioner took a huge step back – falling off the back of the platform behind the gallows – leaving the nooses swinging in front of the two girls. Gwyn looked at Merry who looked at Gwyn and the two girls jumped, ankles still bound, into the yawning space left by the open trapdoor.

Now Ronan of Feldham moved, scrambling across the platform intent on following the girls, while Whitmore tried to placate the crowd – having grabbed hold of the escaping Lord Sherborne by the elbow.

"Come on!" Gabe said, skirting the edge of the crowd, which was now howling and cheering, slapping each other on the backs, as Albert soared once more into the sky. Midge whistled one more time and he disappeared, with a furious, shrieking cry over the castle walls, a flurry of arrows following him.

Eddie and Gabe exchanged looks and, together, they pushed past a rowdy group of stable boys towards the platform. Midge had disappeared and Gabe assumed she was under the platform. Of Scarlett, there was no sign.

A tight phalanx of soldiers, all wearing Lord Sherborne's colors, had surrounded the wooden cage that held Ralf Hodges and the other two prisoners. They stood, backs to the cage, swords held in front of them, at the ready.

Ducking and weaving through the heaving crowd, Gabe made his way steadily in the direction of the platform, ignoring the occasional cuff to the head or blow to the shoulder. He had only one thought in his mind and that was to save Gwyn and Merry.

A red-faced woman in an apron put a hand on his arm.

"Where d'you think you're going?" she screamed in his face, while the heavyset man beside her gulped thirstily from a tankard of ale.

Gabe realized he was now more frightened of the unpredictable nature of the crowd than he was of Lord Sherborne's soldiers. They, at least, did as Lord Sherborne or Whitmore or someone in charge told them to do. But an angry mob fueled by ale . . .

"Good morrow, kind mistress," Eddie said, smoothly, stepping in front of Gabe to bow to the woman. "My friend here has had too much ale and is looking for a quiet place to sleep it off."

He nudged Gabe, who immediately slumped against him as though unwell.

"Well, now, ain't you lah-di-dah 'n' fancy," the woman shrieked, grinning at Eddie and batting her eyelashes. "All right then – let them pass!"

The group standing around the woman suddenly parted, creating a clear path to the front of the crowd for Gabe and Eddie. "Off you go then," the woman said, patting Gabe on the head. "And mind you don't drink any more."

Eddie chuckled, slapping Gabe on the back and propelling him forward. "He won't!" he assured the woman over his shoulder. "Manners," grinned Eddie, as they scrambled under the festive banner that was draped across the front of the platform, mostly to cover up the executioner's work once the hangings were over. "They'll get you everywhere."

The space under the platform was empty.

"Where are they?" hissed Eddie, all joking forgotten.

"I don't know," said Gabe, feeling foolish. Of course, Gwyn and Merry had not waited around to be saved – the girls had done it themselves, as they always did. Worst of all, in his blundering efforts to be a hero, Gabe had ended up right under Lord Sherborne, Whitmore, Ronan of Feldham and Prior Dismas, with the Ateban Cipher stuffed into his breeches.

"We can't stay here," Gabe said, frantically. "We –"

"Oh ho," came a soft voice behind the banner. "I think that here is exactly where you'll stay."

Gabe turned in horror, as Damman, Prior Dismas's favored postulant, ducked in behind the banner.

"Eddie!" Gabe said. "Run!"

"Oh no, you don't," said Damman, reaching out with lightning-quick hands to grab Gabe, forcing him into a headlock. Eddie lunged for the back of the platform, rolling under the banner at the back, and Gabe almost cheered.

His hopes were dashed seconds later by the grunts and thuds of a scuffle, followed by Whitmore's voice. "Ah, the imposter," he said, and Gabe could hear every bit of his sneering satisfaction. "I have you again and this time you will not escape me."

Damman dragged Gabe under the banner to join Whitmore, and Gabe gasped to see Eddie lying still in the dirt, three soldiers standing over him, pointing long, sharp swords at his body.

"Well, well, well, the thief as well," said Whitmore, his dark eyes alight with glee. "It seems my day is turning around."

He turned to the soldiers. "Get him up on the platform," Whitmore said. "The crowd has been robbed of two hangings today . . . but it seems that they will be denied no longer."

As Eddie was dragged away, his head lolling, Gabe struggled in Damman's enveloping, suffocating grasp. "Cut it out!" the larger boy said, punching Gabe in the back of the head so hard he saw stars. "Prior Dismas is going to be so happy to see you." He paused. "And this," he said, reaching under Gabe's tunic and pulling the book out from its hiding place. "Oh yes, he'll definitely be happy to see this." Sniggering, Damman adjusted his grip on Gabe's neck and began to drag him by the heels towards the platform, almost choking him in the process.

All Gabe could do was to stare up at the sky, knowing that he had failed Brother Benedict. Failed Brother Malachy. Failed Lucien.

And, most of all, failed himself.

CHAPTER ELEVEN

Everything looked smaller from up here. The faces in the crowd. The archers on the battlements. Albert circling above.

Everything but the noose, which, close up, looked enormous.

"Are you all right?" Eddie asked him, woozily. Glancing across at him, Gabe could see that Eddie was unsteady on his feet, swaying in time with the swinging noose.

"Honestly," said Gabe. "Not really."

"Me neither," said Eddie, staring out at the crowd, a mass of different hats and hair colors.

Lord Sherborne, Whitmore, Ronan of Feldham and Prior Dismas were huddled together near the platform stairs, presumably gloating over the book, while the executioner went through the motions of retesting the gallows. The trapdoor yawned at Gabe's feet.

"Right then, lads," the executioner said gruffly, but not unkindly, still dusting debris off his breeches. "Here's how it works. I'll set you up in the nooses and then just give you a gentle shove into the trapdoor. It'll be all over before you've had a chance to shout."

He paused. "Unless you struggle," the executioner warned. "Then there's more chance for things to go wrong and when things go wrong, that's when it hurts. Really hurts. I've seen men take hours to die."

Gabe gulped.

"You do realize that you're about to hang the rightful Prince of Alban," said Eddie.

The big man threw back his head and laughed. "Yeah, right, and I'm the King of Caledon. Come on, lads, you looked sensible enough. Don't make it any worse for yourselves. Won't be long now."

With that, he strode off along the platform to signal his readiness to Lord Sherborne.

"Should we jump?" Gabe asked, staring down into the hole at his feet. "It worked for Gwyn and Merry."

"Only because there was someone waiting to help them," Eddie said. "They'll be long gone, Gabe. And why not? Sticking around here drastically shortens your life."

Gabe's eyes scanned the crowd, searching for a sign of the girls. "They won't abandon us," he said.

"They won't want to," corrected Eddie. "But what's the point in all of us dying here today? You've got to admit they take a practical approach to most things."

Gabe could only nod, and then the executioner was suddenly looming over him once more.

"It's time," he said, quietly, and Gabe bowed his head, unable to think straight anymore.

Lord Sherborne stepped forward. "We promised you a hanging and by Jove a hanging we shall have!" he shouted, and the crowd cheered, having forgotten their unrest and upheaval in the face of a public spectacle.

"So . . . without further ado," Lord Sherborne said. "I sentence these two to be hanged."

"For what?" shouted a man's voice from the crowd.

"Oh, yes, er, thievery, public unrest and treason," said Lord Sherborne, as though reading a shopping list. He stepped back to stand beside the fake Prince, who was still lolling on his throne as though asleep.

"Right then," said the executioner, taking the rope and dropping the noose over Gabe's head, where it landed, thick and scratchy, on his shoulders. Gabe staggered, as though a great weight had settled on him, and the executioner grabbed his shoulder to steady him.

"Wait for your friend," he said to Gabe. "Won't be long."

He stepped across to drop the noose around Eddie's neck, as Eddie cursed him loudly. "Now, now, just doing my job," the executioner said, as the crowd in the front row laughed.

But as he gathered Eddie's rope into his huge hands, the executioner suddenly stepped back with an oath. Gabe's eyes widened as he realized the man had an arrow stuck in his arm! The crowd gasped, ducking for cover, as arrows began to rain down on the platform, one after the other – this one landing in the rope above Gabe's head, splitting it neatly, that one dropping at Lord Sherborne's feet, a finger width from the toe of his boot.

The executioner threw himself to the ground behind Eddie, who jumped across on his bound feet to stand beside Gabe.

"Don't move!" Gabe shouted. "It's Merry. If you don't move, she won't hit us!"

"How do you know?" Eddie asked, face white with fear. "I can't even see where they're coming from!"

"The arrows," said Gabe, ducking down and bending forward to try to remove the noose from his neck. "They're hers!"

"We can't just stand here," said Eddie. "Look at them!"

He gestured to the crowd, which was now a heaving mass of people trying to escape as the archers on the battlements began to loosen arrows every which way. They couldn't see Merry, Gabe realized, so they were randomly firing off shots in panic.

"We're not going to just stand here," Gabe said, face red with the effort of trying to shake the noose off. "Can you get this rope off me?"

Eddie turned around and using both hands behind him, managed to slip the noose over Gabe's head without removing his ears.

"Phew," said Gabe, standing up. "Thanks. It wasn't the most comfortable thing I've ever worn."

"But it looked so good on you," came a voice from their feet, and Gabe looked down to see Gwyn grinning up at them mischievously through the trapdoor. "Do you want to get yourselves down here so that I can get those ropes off you, Sandals?"

"Go on, Gabe," said Eddie, casting a nervous glance at the other end of the platform where Lord Sherborne and the others were still cowering, while shouting orders at their soldiers. Gabe noticed that Prior Dismas was hiding behind the throne, while the fake Prince had not moved.

Suddenly, a commotion erupted at the gates and Gabe froze as a gray-haired soldier in royal colors came flying into the courtyard on a huge, snorting charger, the metal of its horseshoes clanging on the cobblestones. The crowd – already roiling with panic and fear – seemed to hold its collective breath for a tiny moment, before every man, woman and child began to run for the nearest gate.

"STOP IN THE NAME OF THE KING," roared the soldier, resplendent in purple, his magnificent white horse gleaming.

It was as though time stood still – every person froze in a tableau of horror.

"Jump, Gabe!" hissed Gwyn, but Gabe was staring out over the crowd, watching in disbelief as a dozen more soldiers rode into the courtyard, keeping such a close formation that they looked like a one-legged animal.

They came to a halt behind the white charger and for a moment nobody moved.

"Ah!" said Whitmore, stepping forward into the silence, and Gabe was surprised to hear a tiny hint of nervousness in the sound. "Sir Henry, finally back from your quest . . . As you can see, all is well here, the Prince is in residence." He waved a hand in the direction of the throne. "We are, of course, here on behalf of the King and we are hanging thieves and traitors in his name." Whitmore's voice gained confidence as he spoke.

"Are you now?" said Sir Henry, a smirk on his face, his horse dancing beneath him, tapping on the cobblestones. He turned as the gates opened once more and an ornate, golden carriage rolled sedately through them.

"That's my father's carriage," said Eddie, sounding alarmed. "What new trick is this?"

Whitmore's face went white and Lord Sherborne seemed to shrink.

"We'll just ask him about that then, shall we?" said Sir Henry, clearly enjoying himself.

"Father," breathed Eddie, and would have stepped forward into the trapdoor had Gabe not put out both hands to stop him. "But how?"

The carriage rolled to a stop and two footmen jumped off the back, placing a short roll of tapestry on the cobblestones before pulling down the step and opening the door with a flourish. After a short pause, the King emerged from the plush velvet interior, leaning heavily on his servant, Purvis.

"Oh Father," whispered Eddie, taking in the King's pale, clammy face.

"It seems the King has been unwell in my absence," said Sir Henry at the King's signal. "But he's feeling much better now and he's come to see his son."

"Oh, he's quite, quite well," said Lord Sherborne, wringing his hands together as he bowed before the King. "See?"

The imposter lolled on his throne, unmoved by events around him. Prior Dismas whispered to him and he waved.

"Excellent," said Sir Henry. "Then we shall look forward to enjoying your Winterfest celebrations with you. I assume that all this –" He waved his hand at the empty nooses, an expression of distaste on his face, "– is over?"

Whitmore smiled. "Well, we were just about to, er –"

The soldier stared at Whitmore, but the King looked up at the platform, his eyes taking in both boys, standing bound hand and foot.

"It's over," the King said, his voice weak but certain. "There will be no hangings today. Send everyone to your Great Hall for the feast."

Gabe nearly fell to his knees on the platform, so great was his relief.

"We shall retreat to your solar, Lord Sherborne," said the King, and while his voice was not strong, Gabe noticed that his gaze, as he looked past Whitmore to Lord Sherborne, was sharp. "Assuming it is still yours?"

At his words, Whitmore flushed, his eyes narrowed with rage, but he stepped back, allowing Lord Sherborne to take center stage.

"Welcome, Your Majesty," Sherborne said, bowing so low his nose almost touched the platform. "We are truly honored by your visit."

But the King was frowning at the lethargic figure on the throne. "Edward!" he called out.

"Your son has been under the weather," said Sherborne, smoothly. "He is under the care of Prior Dismas from Oldham Abbey, a great center for healing as you know. I'm sure he'll, er, perk up once we get him inside out of the cold."

Gabe watched as Prior Dismas and Damman hauled the fake Prince to his feet, and all but dragged him off the platform, Prior Dismas whispering to Damman the whole time.

"Shall we?" Lord Sherborne asked, indicating that the King should follow, his smile forced. Gabe wondered if anyone else had noticed Ronan of Feldham edge down the stairs, his eyes on Damman and Prior Dismas.

"We shall," said the King. "Indeed, we shall."

He turned to the gray-haired soldier. "Bring those two, Henry," he said, pointing a bejeweled hand at Gabe and Eddie. "I have some questions for them."

Gabe gulped, even as Eddie brightened beside him.

"And the other prisoners?" Sherborne enquired politely, though Gabe could hear the grit beneath his words.

"What other prisoners?" Henry asked, mildly.

"Wha–" Sherborne turned to the wooden cage, which was now empty. The door, littered with crossbow bolts, hung drunkenly to one side.

"It seems we have just the two to deal with," said the King, firmly. "Lead on, Sherborne. There is much to discuss."

As a soldier cut the cords that bound him, and indicated that Gabe should follow Henry, Gabe felt as though he was simply going from the blacksmith's anvil into the fire. He had seen the way the King's hard stare had lingered on his face, and he knew that the King had seen in him exactly what Aurora and Lucien had seen – a strong resemblance to Dylan.

The more he thought about it, the more Gabe realized that it was this that had caused the King to faint in his bedchamber, setting off this entire chain of events, and causing Gabe to lose the Ateban Cipher.

With all that in mind, and given the King's feelings for his father, left to rot in a dungeon, Gabe wasn't feeling hopeful about his own future.

"You are looking well, Sire," said Lord Sherborne, casting a look at Whitmore. "Very well, indeed."

"Yes," said the King, settling back into the velvet cushions that had been arranged on a magnificent carved timber chair for him, his face revealing nothing. "I feel better today than I have in many months. Strange, when I missed all meals yesterday and breakfast this morning."

Purvis, standing behind the King, raised his eyebrows at Whitmore, a small smile playing about his lips.

"Yes," the King said, playing with the thick, gold chain that encircled his waist. "Quite by chance, Henry here returned from many months in the East, to find me most unwell. It was he who suggested that perhaps not eating might be better for my health. It seems he had seen my, er, symptoms on other occasions whilst away. What do you think about that, Whitmore?"

"Er, very strange indeed, Sire," said Whitmore through thin lips, while Henry stood solidly beside his King.

"And yet," the King continued, still not looking at his head guard, "Purvis here fed my meals to his cat – so as not to waste them, you understand – and today, the poor cat is unable to raise her head."

Whitmore spluttered but seemed unable to answer.

"Goodness me," said Lord Sherborne, stepping into the conversation, trying to sound sincere. "How fortunate that you didn't eat those meals. It's almost as though they were . . . poisoned."

A heavy silence fell over the room.

"Indeed," said the King, eventually.

"And yet, here you are in the very bloom of health," said Lord Sherborne, trying to sound jolly. "Back with your son."

He dropped an arm around the shoulders of the fake Prince, who said nothing.

"Edward," said the King, turning his attention to the boy. "You have hardly said a word since I arrived. Come here and sit beside your father."

He gestured to the fake Prince, who did not move.

"Ah," said Prior Dismas, sounding nervous. "He has been unwell, Your Majesty, as you know. He has a sore throat and cannot speak."

The King frowned and opened his mouth to speak, but Eddie had had enough.

"That's because he's not the Prince!" he announced. "I am the Prince."

"Oh, not this again," said Lord Sherborne, rolling his eyes. "My apologies, Your Majesty, this boy is addled in the head." He turned to a heavyset soldier, wearing the red livery of the House of Sherborne. "Get him out of here!" he demanded.

"No," said the King, quietly. "He stays." He waved Eddie forward. "Come here, boy. Let me get a good look at you."

It was only as he said this that Gabe realized just how different Eddie looked from the smooth, polished Prince he'd been when they'd first met eight weeks earlier. Then, his hair had been trim, his face clean, his cheeks full. Just as the fake Prince's was now.

But now Eddie was covered in dirt, his wild hair was long enough to reach his shoulders and the breeches and tunic that he'd been eating, sleeping and traveling in for weeks were torn, stained and, Gabe thought wrinkling his nose, more than a little bit smelly.

No wonder his own father was having trouble recognizing him.

"Father," Eddie said, throwing himself at the King's feet.

The King frowned, looking from Eddie's hunched form to the fake Prince. "The resemblance between these two is uncanny. But you say this one is a simpleton?"

Lord Sherborne sighed. "We believe so," he said. "He was caught poaching in the forest and, whilst in my dungeons, appears to have convinced himself that he is the Crown Prince."

"That's because I am!" shouted Eddie in anguish. "Father, look at me!"

His father peered down at him. "Purvis, get him cleaned up," he said. "I can't see anything under that layer of grime."

Eddie allowed himself to be led away, and the room waited in silence. When Eddie returned fifteen minutes later, even Gabe was startled by the change in him. His hair had been brushed back from his face, which was now clean, and Purvis had even managed to rustle up a new set of clothes, which were much more in keeping with a noble household.

"Ah," said the King. "I see. Remarkable. They could be twins."

"Yes, *he* looks like *me*," said Eddie, with a haughty look at the fake Prince.

"And yet," said Lord Sherborne, "he bears the mark."

"*I* bear the mark!" said Eddie.

"So you've said," said Lord Sherborne, dismissively, "but this is the Prince who stepped out of the royal carriage on his arrival at Rothwell. While you . . ." He paused dramatically, pointing at Eddie. "You disrupted the melee with your outrageous claim."

"Because it's true!" shouted Eddie. "And you know it."

The King shook his head, bewildered, and Gabe could see that, despite his rapid recovery on the surface, the King's thoughts were still confused. "How can there be two of you?" he said.

"There aren't," said Eddie. "There is only me."

"Um," said Gabe, almost without thinking. "Perhaps you could ask them some questions, Your, er, Majesty."

He stopped as all eyes in the room turned to him. "Er, things that only the real Prince would know."

Prior Dismas glared at him. "The Prince is in no fit state to answer questions," he said. "His throat . . ."

Lord Sherborne smiled silkily. "Perhaps he could whisper the answers to you and you could relay them to the rest of us," he said, with a meaningful look at Prior Dismas. Gabe sighed, realizing that Sherborne had been prepared for something like this. Or, more likely, Prior Dismas had been prepared – by Whitmore, no doubt.

But the King nodded. "Very well," he said. "Let us begin."

Ten minutes later, Gabe was beginning to despair. Prior Dismas had answered every single one of the King's questions, right down to the special lullaby that the King had sung to the baby Prince, and his answers were identical to Eddie's. The Prior would pretend to consult with the fake Prince while Eddie answered the question, and then would simply give the same answer. Even when required to answer first, the Prior would simply smirk and give the correct response. Whitmore had clearly schooled him well on the details of Eddie's daily life in the castle as well as royal protocol in case a day such as this ever arose.

What they needed, Gabe thought, was a question that only Eddie would know – something that the Prior couldn't have learned through Whitmore or his other sources. "I have a question," he said, slowly, raising his hand. Eddie frowned at him, and Gabe tried to look confident.

The King sighed. "Very well," he said. "But this is the last one."

Gabe gulped, as Eddie went pale. "Don't you recognize me, Father?" he whispered.

The King gave him a long look, his expression regally blank. "If you are the real Prince you will know that the royal lineage is no place for games or doubt and the Prince has many here who vouch for him. You will also know that what I want or think as King is bound by duty and protocol. *He* is the one who stepped from the royal carriage. He *is* the one who has the endorsement of the Prince's personal guard, entrusted beyond all others to protect him. *You* are the one that must prove otherwise, and prove it beyond all doubt."

Eddie bit his lip, blinking back tears, and Gabe thought he would shout and scream. But he simply stepped back, nodding once, while Whitmore and Sherborne tried hard to contain their glee.

"Ask your question, er . . ." the King looked at Gabe.

"Gabe," said Gabe, not leaving his place beside the wall. "Well, it's a simple question, but I have one request."

"Yes, yes, what is it?" asked the King.

"I would like the Prince to answer first," he said, bowing his head in the direction of the imposter.

The King considered Gabe for a long moment. "Very well," he said, and Gabe could see Prior Dismas shift uncomfortably as all eyes turned to him and the imposter.

Gabe didn't even look at Eddie as he spoke. "Where are the spare keys to the royal castle kept?" he asked.

Prior Dismas laughed, before hurriedly pretending to listen to the fake Prince's whispered answer. Gabe had noticed that he always dipped his head across the Prince's face when he did this, shielding from the King the fact that the fake Prince's lips didn't move.

The Prior raised his head, a triumphant smile on his face. "In the castle strongbox, of course," he said.

Gabe glanced at the King, whose countenance did not change as he nodded at Eddie.

Eddie caught and held his father's gaze. "The keys are kept in the larder," he said.

"Bah!" said Whitmore, as Lord Sherborne rocked with laughter. "Answered like the true peasant you are! Guards, seize him!"

But the King, still staring into Eddie's face, raised one hand and everyone in the room stilled.

"This boy is correct. This boy is my son," he said, nodding at Eddie, and Gabe could see a glimmering of relief under his royal composure. He'd known all along, Gabe realized, as Eddie knelt before the King and received his father's hand on his shoulder. To protect the throne, however, the whole room had to know the truth beyond any question.

"Guards," the King said, without raising his voice, "seize them."

Suddenly, the room erupted as Lord Sherborne, Whitmore and Prior Dismas realized that the game was up. Whitmore drew his sword while Sherborne shrieked for his personal soldiers. Prior Dismas dropped to his knees, shaking and weeping.

But it was too late for all of them, and the royal soldiers quickly overpowered and bound them, before leading them away.

"What about him?" Eddie asked, nodding at the fake Prince, who still had not moved.

"It's not his fault," said Gabe, coming to stand beside Eddie. "Look at him! He's still drugged. Chances are that he knows nothing of all this."

The King nodded. "Your friend is right," he said. "We will send him to the nearest infirmarium to recover and then back to his home, wherever that may be. He will probably have no memory at all of his time on the 'throne.'"

"Brother Archibold at Oldham Abbey will look after him," said Gabe, as two soldiers stepped forward to carry out the King's wishes. They picked up the fake Prince and carried him from the room, his feet dragging behind them.

"Father," said Eddie, "I am so glad to see you well. When you collapsed in the solar . . ." His words trailed away. "How did you know to come here?"

"Ah yes," said the King, turning to Gabe. "I followed the painting. When the painting disappeared and Whitmore went tearing off at first light, Henry and I put two and two together. So perhaps I followed Whitmore more than the painting, but the result is the same."

"The painting?" questioned Gabe.

The King frowned. "Surely it was you who took it. I saw your eyes and thought . . ."

Gabe nodded, understanding. "It wasn't me who took it, but I know why you might have thought that."

"You're Dylan's son," said the King, sounding tired. "Dylan and Aurora. When I saw your eyes, I knew and I . . ." He paused before taking a long, shaky breath. "I've made some mistakes," he continued, eyes on Gabe. "I was younger, foolish. Lucien told me that I didn't realize what truly mattered and he was right. Once I did, it was too late. Dylan was dead, Lucien was angry, Aurora was gone. I couldn't see how anyone would forgive me."

He paused, seemingly deep in thought. "I kept the painting to remind me," he said. "When I woke up this morning and it was gone, it was as though the past had come back to haunt me."

The King looked at Gabe. "I need it back," he said, simply. "Now that you are here, I need it more than ever."

"I had it, but Prior Dismas took it from me," said Gabe, not really understanding why the painting was so important. Surely it could be painted again?

The King nodded at Henry, who left the room.

"Did you notice anything taped to the back?" the King asked, urgently.

"Yes," said Eddie. "A letter with your seal. I thought it strange. What is it?"

The King put a hand on Gabe's shoulder. "It is the true story of your birth," he said. "Your claim to the throne should anything happen to me or to Eddie."

Gabe felt faint. "The throne?" he gasped.

Eddie laughed. "Well, yes," he said. "Didn't you make that connection? If Aurora is your mother, then I am your cousin and you are next in line to the throne after me."

Gabe felt his legs go out from under him, and he landed on his breeches on the thick carpet. "I didn't think of that," he said, truthfully. "I'm not really cut out to be a Prince."

The King laughed. "Don't worry," he said. "It may never happen. And you'll be trained."

"Um, Sire," said Gabe, feeling sick. "I'd rather not if that's all right. I just want to go back to my life as it was before."

Eddie sat down on the rug beside him. "But that's not possible," he said, gently. "Not now."

Gabe was saved from answering when Henry burst back through the door, holding a painting in one hand – and a squirming Gwyn in the other.

"I found the painting," he said, his face blank, though Gabe could see his lips twitching. "And I found this . . . person listening outside the door." He all but dropped Gwyn on the floor beside Gabe.

Eddie laughed. "There'll be three others out there in the hallway," he told his father. "You might as well invite them all in now."

He stood up and strode to the door, opening it so quickly that Merry, Scarlett and Midge nearly fell through it.

"This," said Eddie, moving to put one hand on Gwyn's shoulder, "is your thief. She stole your painting."

Gwyn muttered something unsavory under her breath at Eddie for giving her up, but the King simply smiled. "I have you to thank for bringing me here," he said to Gwyn, who was shocked into silence.

Not so Merry. "Good," she said, bouncing over to bow before the King. "Does that mean you owe her one?"

The King looked bemused. "I suppose it does," he said, slowly.

"Lovely," said Merry, her eyes dancing. "Then perhaps you could organize a royal pardon for our father, Ralf Hodges?"

The King turned to look at Henry, who was still trying to suppress a grin. "Ralf Hodges?"

"He was accused of killing your royal stag, Your Highness," Merry interjected before Henry could speak. "But seeing as Gwyn, Midge and Gabe found the stag alive and well and in the hands of one of Whitmore's cronies,

I'm thinking that the charges should be dropped. Eddie will confirm the details."

"Eddie?" said the King, faintly, blanching at the casual nickname.

"Eddie," Prince Edward confirmed with a smile. "And she's telling the truth."

"Well, I see no reason not to pardon, er, Ralf, then," said the King, leaning back in his chair. "See that he's released, Henry."

"Oh, he's already released," said Gwyn, from her seated position. "We saw to that, just in case. We just need the piece of vellum to make it official."

"Very well," said the King, with a tiny smile. "Henry, see to the, er, piece of vellum, will you?"

Henry smiled. "With pleasure, Sire," he said.

"Is that everything?" the King asked Merry. "Er, Miss Hodges?"

"Merry," said Merry, with a wink. "Well, there is the matter of Scarlett."

"Scarlett?" asked the King.

"That's me," said Scarlett, stepping forward, swinging her braid back over her shoulder. In the sumptuous surrounds of Lord Sherborne's parlor, she should have looked out of place in her dirty breeches, and yet she looked right at home amongst the velvets, silks and satins.

"And you are?" said the King.

"Scarlett Montledge of Tayston," she said, fifteen years of noble breeding coming to the fore in her rounded vowels and intonation. Gabe remembered how he'd told her not to speak the first day they'd gone to Rothwell Castle, and now he remembered why. He'd become so used to the sound of her voice and the beauty of her face that he had stopped noticing either.

"I see," said the King. "And how may I help you, young lady?"

"It's my father, Sire," she said. "He wishes me to marry Lord Havering Kenson."

There was a pause. "And you do not wish this to be the case?" the King asked. "You want to go against your father's wishes?"

Scarlett hesitated, and Gabe knew she was treading on dangerous ground. A daughter was her father's property, and it was up to him to decide how best to use her to further the family's fortunes.

"I wish for more time to decide," Scarlett said, carefully, with a dazzling smile that made her blue eyes sparkle.

"Hmmmm," said the King, his fingers steepled before him.

Henry leaned over to whisper in his ear, and the King nodded. "What say we do this," he said to Scarlett. "I will make you a ward of my court for one year, keeping you under my care and protection, at no expense to your father. If, at the end of that time, he still wishes to marry you to Lord Kenson, then you will accept his decision."

Gabe wondered about the last, but Scarlett glowed with pleasure. "Oh, thank you, Sire," she said, before stepping back beside Merry.

"Father will be thrilled," he heard her mutter to Merry. "My prospects will increase threefold at court and he will deem Lord Kenson to be unworthy."

Gabe blinked, not only at the assessment but at Scarlett's understanding of familial and courtly politics.

"And what of you?" the King asked, turning to Midge, who stood quietly beside Merry, watching everything with her big brown eyes.

"Oh, I'm very happy," she said now to the King. "I'll stay with Merry and Gwyn and Albert."

"Albert?" the King asked, looking pained. "Who is Albert? Is he waiting outside in the hallway?"

"Oh no," Midge said with a giggle. "He's just outside the window there."

Sure enough, Albert was perched on the windowsill, peering intently into the room through the thick glass, beady eyes ever-watchful, ever-protective of his friend.

The King looked nonplussed.

"And our pa, of course," said Merry, seeming to realize that most people wouldn't consider a peregrine falcon a suitable guardian for a young girl. "He'll be back with us now."

235

"Yes," said the King, looking more relaxed at the idea of an adult being in charge. Gabe smiled to himself, wondering how Eddie's father would react if they told him the full story of the girls' years in the forest.

"Well," the King went on. "That would seem to be everything then. Edward . . ."

He reached out a hand to Eddie, who took it. "We'll need to stay here a day or two. Lord Sherborne's books require a thorough audit and I would like Henry to oversee the removal of him and the other prisoners to Callchester Castle."

"Yes, Father," said Eddie. "You'll need to rest up and get your strength back as well."

"Indeed," said the King with a sigh, and Gabe could see the white lines around his mouth.

"But," Gabe said, unable to help himself, "what about the book?"

The King frowned. "The book?"

"Yes," said Gabe, looking at Henry. "Wasn't there a book with the painting?"

Henry shook his head slowly. "No book," he said. "I found the painting in Lord Sherborne's solar, but there were no books in there at all. Not so much as a bible."

"It must have been there!" said Gabe, striding towards the door, his scalp prickling. "He took it at the same time!"

"Who took it?" asked the King. "What is the book?"

Gabe turned, worry making him forget that he was talking to the most important man in Alban. "The Ateban Cipher!" he shouted. "Prior Dismas took it from me when they were going to –"

Gabe was suddenly overcome with that same feeling he'd had watching that huge noose swaying before him.

"The Ateban Cipher?" said the King, sinking back onto his cushions, eyes wide. "It's real?"

Eddie nodded. "I've seen it," he said. "Lucien told us what it was."

"I thought it was just a story," the King said, looking dazed. "The Book of Answers . . ." His voice trailed away as he stared over their heads for a moment. "And now it's gone?" the King continued, sitting forward again, eyebrows knitted. "Taken from you?"

Gabe could only stare at the floor. "Stolen," he said, trying to think. "It could be anywhere. Anyone could have it. And it's all my fault."

The King cleared his throat. "Gabe," he said, but whatever he was about to say next was drowned out in a clatter of horses' hooves and shouting in the courtyard.

"Henry, what *is* that racket?" the King asked, turning to his guard.

But it was Midge by the window who answered, nose pressed against the glass. "Borlan!" she shouted. "It's Borlan!"

"Who the devil is Borlan?" the King spluttered as Merry, Gwyn, Midge and Scarlett all dashed from the room without so much as a by-your-leave.

"Not who," laughed Eddie. "*What*. Borlan is a horse."

"A horse?" said the King, with a shake of his head, while Henry chuckled.

"Yes," said Eddie, "and the big question is what the devil he's doing here!"

Eddie ran from the room after the girls, leaving an aching Gabe to follow slowly behind. He'd be happy to see Borlan again, Gabe thought, happy to return him to Oldham Abbey where he belonged.

But he wished Borlan wasn't the only thing being safely returned to the Abbey.

CHAPTER TWELVE

Once outside in the courtyard, even Gabe couldn't help but smile at the joyous scene. Midge was sitting atop the giant stallion, draped over his neck, her cheek between his ears. If Borlan had been a cat, Gabe thought, he would have been purring. Jasper and Bess stood quietly behind him, kept close on the long tether that Nicholas had used to lead them behind Borlan.

A crowd from the Great Hall had gathered at a safe distance to admire the gleaming horse, steam rising from his satiny coat in the cold air. Nicholas pumped Eddie's hand in greeting, before pulling the girls towards him for a group hug – not the first, judging by Gwyn's expression as Nicholas dragged them in.

"Ah, Gabe," Nicholas said, catching his eye over Merry's flaming curls, "it's so good to see you. When the stable man at Callchester told me what had happened I came as fast as I could!"

"Thanks," said Gabe, trying to look pleased to see him. The truth was, he could think of little else but the lost book, and wondered if it would always be that way now.

"But you're all okay!" Nicholas said, looking around with a grin spreading across his homely face, even as he hugged the girls again. "I was worried you'd all be –"

"Dead?" Gwyn finished for him, finally managing to disentangle herself from his enthusiastic greeting. "It was a distinct possibility."

"Yes," said Nicholas, letting her go. "And then when I saw Damman on the road in such a hurry, well, let's just say that it was a good thing Borlan was in a good mood today and happy enough to let me shout at him to go faster."

He chattered on, but Gabe had stopped listening. "Damman?" he said, slowly, walking over to grip Nicholas by the arm. "On the road?"

"Yes," said Nicholas, with a puzzled glance at Gabe. "I don't think I've ever seen him move so fast. Didn't know he could, to be honest. That weaselly face of his all screwed up with effort –"

"Which way?" said Gabe, cutting off Nicholas's anecdote, suddenly remembering Prior Dismas and Damman with their heads together as they dragged the fake Prince from the platform. "Was he carrying anything?"

Nicholas stared at him thoughtfully. "I don't think . . ." he began, before stopping, biting his lip. "Wait, no, he was wearing his robes, kept clutching at his pocket. You know how you do when you're trying to stop something from falling out?"

Gabe nodded. The robes he had worn at Oldham Abbey for most of his life had deep pockets. He had kept the book in one of them himself when he'd first fled into the forest. And, Gabe remembered, hadn't he kept checking constantly to make sure it was still there?

"Was he alone?" asked Merry, and Gabe became aware that all the girls were listening intently.

Nicholas shook his head. "No, I don't think so," he said. "There was a man striding ahead of him. Big man, all brown, looked like he was carved of wood. Damman was doing his best to keep up with him."

"Ronan of Feldham . . . They've got the book," said Gabe, never surer of anything in his life. "Prior Dismas gave it to Damman and told him to take it – but he was followed by Ronan. We need to get it back."

Gwyn nodded. "I'll go," she said, already detaching herself from the group. "I'll bring it back to the Abbey."

The King raised his eyebrows at Henry, who frowned, gray moustache bristling.

"Take Jasper," Nicholas said, his eyes on Gwyn. "Head south. Past Oldham Abbey, on the Callchester Road."

Henry stepped forward, all his years of soldiering experience in his authoritative stance. "I really think this is a task for someone . . . older," he said.

But Eddie put a hand on his father's arm. "Gwyn can do it," he said. "Really."

The King gave his son a long look before sighing. "Very well," he said, signaling Henry to stand down. "You know more about all this than I do. The girl can go, Henry."

"Not without me," said Gabe, following Gwyn, who hadn't even acknowledged the conversation about her.

Now Gwyn stopped, turning to look at Gabe, hands on hips, though her face was impassive. "I'll be faster without you, Sandals," she said, calmly. "You know I will."

Gabe nodded. "Perhaps," he said, blushing when she cocked her head, eyes challenging. "Okay, definitely, but I'm the keeper of the book. I lost it. It's up to me to get it back."

Gwyn stared at him for a long moment. "All right," she said, turning on her heel. "If you can keep up, you can come."

"Good luck, Gabe!" Merry called out, and Gabe could hear an undertone of laughter in her voice. "Oh wait, you might need this."

He turned, and she tossed her precious longbow towards him. A moment later, a quiver full of arrows landed at his feet.

"Thank you," Gabe said, quietly, as he picked them up. In trusting him with her precious weapon, Merry was offering him much more than simply a means of protection or defense, she was giving him her confidence and respect, two things he had only dreamed of gaining just a few short months ago.

"Come on, Sandals," said Gwyn, already astride Jasper. "Your friend Damman is not going to wait for us."

"He's not my friend," Gabe said, climbing up behind her, and settling the longbow across his lap.

Gwyn merely chuckled in response.

Putting his arms around her waist, Gabe held on for dear life as she dug her heels into Jasper's side, and the horse responded immediately, lunging forward as though anticipating the thrill of the chase.

Gabe could only wish he felt the same, but the truth was that he was equal parts anxious, worried and terrified of Damman. The bigger boy was wily and mean, used to pushing people around to get what he wanted.

Ronan of Feldham he couldn't even think about.

"Relax, Sandals," Gwyn said, without looking at him. "You're going to upset Jasper if you sit there all stiff and nervy. And your arrows will be useless if you can't control your feelings."

With a deep sigh, Gabe did his best to do as she said, watching the trees pass in a blur as Jasper's long legs ate up the miles along the dusty road.

❖

"You know what to do?"

Gabe nodded, then, realizing that Gwyn wouldn't be able to see the movement in the darkness, whispered, "Yes."

"Don't try to get fancy," she warned. "Stick to the plan. Ronan of Feldham is not likely to give up easily."

"I don't want to kill him," Gabe said, worried.

Gwyn chuckled, a faint gurgle in the night air. "Then don't," she said. "Aim high. All we want to do is to separate him from Damman long enough to take the book back. Then we run as fast as we can back to the Abbey. They don't have a horse and they're not likely to turn up at the Abbey accusing us of stealing it now, are they?"

Gabe shook his head. Her plan was simple, as her plans often were. His job was to keep Ronan pinned to one spot with arrows while Gwyn went after Damman. "He'll run," she'd said, confidently, when she'd outlined her idea. "As soon as you start shooting, he'll duck for cover and I'll be after him."

Poor Damman, Gabe had thought, *not realizing that the arrows were the least of his worries . . .*

"Okay," Gwyn said now. "I'm going. Don't move until you hear the signal."

With that, she was gone and Gabe could hear nothing but a slight rustling as she moved from tree trunk to tree trunk, working her way around to the other side of the clearing. Frost had made the ground crunchy beneath his feet, but Gwyn seemed to skate over it – *or fly*, he thought to himself. And while many of the trees had dropped their leaves for winter, the trunks were packed closely enough together to provide cover.

Even so, Gabe was happy that the barren branches of the brambles in front of him had twisted and turned and woven themselves into a tight thicket, providing a thick wall between him and the two figures huddled beside a tiny fire at the very center of the clearing.

Damman, the smaller of the two figures, glanced over his shoulder, a nervous, catlike gesture that he repeated often. Gabe knew that the postulant was jumping at every tiny sound, just as Gabe had done on his first night in the forest. Ronan of Feldham cuffed Damman over the back of the head.

"What are you looking at, you foolish boy?" he growled.

"I thought I heard something," Damman said.

"An owl? A squirrel?" said Ronan, and Gabe could almost hear the man rolling his eyes. "Nobody knows we're here, and we'll be gone by first light. The sooner we sell that damn book the sooner we can be rid of it – and each other."

Damman's face was ghostly in the flickering light, as he shivered in his woolen robes, despite the fact that he was almost sitting on the fire. "Prior Dismas told me to hide it at Oldham Abbey," he said, staring at the ground.

"Yes, well, as I told you," said Ronan, and Damman winced at the menace in his voice, "Prior Dismas doesn't make the rules anymore. I do. And I say that we get what we can for a book that no one can read."

He stretched back, his thick cloak wrapped snugly around him. "In fact," the sheriff said, with a yawn, "I think we can get more for the illustrations separately than for the whole book. We'll rip it apart and sell it off, page by page."

Gabe felt cold inside at the very thought of the book being destroyed. He clutched the longbow in fingers that were suddenly stiff, and watched his breath cloud on the cold night air. The wait for Gwyn's signal felt interminable.

At last Gabe heard it, the long, low hissing screech of a barn owl, and raised the bow into position, trying not to notice how hard his hands were shaking. Nocking an arrow, he peered down its shaft, trying to remember everything Merry had taught him.

"Don't focus on the target," she'd said, over and over. "Choose a tiny detail."

That was easier said than done in the firelight – especially when Gabe didn't really want to hit the target at all! In the end, he narrowed his gaze on a white trunk in the tree line behind Ronan of Feldham. If he aimed for that, the arrows should whizz by the sheriff without actually hitting him.

He took a deep breath, awaiting the sharp *pip-pip* call of an alarmed robin – and when it came, released his first arrow without allowing himself to think, not stopping to watch as it flew through the clearing and landed with a thud in the center of the white tree trunk. Gabe heard

Damman's shout as Ronan got to his feet, but Gabe didn't react, instead reaching for another arrow, trying to keep his breath steady.

Merry had always said that the very worst thing an archer could do was to overthink and Gabe was praying that she was right.

Ronan reached for his sword, peering out into the darkness, his face black with menace and rage. But Damman reacted exactly as Gwyn had predicted, crashing off into the shrubs, trying to take cover in the forest.

Gabe allowed himself a small smile, knowing that Damman didn't stand a chance and that Gwyn would have the book within her grasp in minutes, but he didn't take his eyes off the clearing.

Which meant he didn't miss the moment when Ronan, sword drawn, began to advance towards the brambles where Gabe was hidden. Letting loose another arrow, Gabe began to back away, but Ronan continued to advance, his rough-hewn face set in grim lines.

"I know you're there," Ronan growled. "And given I'm not dead, I can only assume you're not man enough to kill me. But do not imagine for a moment that I won't kill you when I catch you. And I *will* catch you."

Gabe gasped, feeling dread rising up from his gut. He scrabbled backward, hampered by the longbow and the quiver of Merry's arrows. His instinct was to drop both and run, but he couldn't bear the thought of returning to her without them, not when she'd trusted him so.

"Cat got your tongue, little rabbit," Ronan said, with a low, maniacal laugh.

He would follow Gabe forever, Gabe realized, his mouth dry. Through the trees, through the darkness, and if he caught Gabe, he would kill him.

And then he'd kill Gwyn.

It was how the world, this world, worked, and no matter what Gabe did or said, no matter how much he wrestled with the good and the bad of it, it was simply what would happen. Unless Gabe did something to stop Ronan of Feldham right now, both he and Gwyn would die. And there was no way Gabe was going to let Gwyn die. Not after everything she'd done for him.

A strange sense of calm came over Gabe as he suddenly changed direction, crawling back towards his bramble hidey-hole, directly in the path of Ronan of Feldham.

"I know you're out there, little rabbit," the man said, his voice now a guttural growl. "Run, rabbit, run."

Every part of Gabe wanted to follow those instructions, as the hair on his arms stood up. Instead, he once again set the longbow to his shoulder and nocked an arrow, praying with everything he had that all the practice Merry had made him do along the road, weeks and weeks of early mornings, would pay off.

Squinting down the arrow in the firelight, Gabe suddenly rose from the brambles, thrusting upward to stand, as steadily as he could, in the stance he'd practiced so many times.

"Oh ho!" said the sheriff, a wide, ugly smile twisting his face as he raised his sword.

Gabe tried not to blink as the sword flashed in the firelight. Instead, he breathed out as slowly as he could and aimed his arrow – down, down, down, focusing on the buckle on the side of Ronan's boot.

And then, before the sheriff could take another step, Gabe let the arrow fly. With a whispered "sorry," he watched as it flew straight and true, into the sheriff's ankle, just as he'd seen Merry do all those months ago on the Rothwell Road.

With a loud curse, Ronan dropped his sword, crouching to his ankle, and Gabe took the opportunity to scramble backward through the brambles. He jumped to his feet, slung the longbow over his shoulder and ran for the trees, aiming for the road where Gwyn had left Jasper.

"Well, well, well," said Gwyn, stepping out from behind a huge ash, leaving Gabe gasping. "Sandals, you surprise me. Who'd have thought?"

"Did you get it?" Gabe asked, ignoring her comments, even though a small part of him glowed at the faint praise.

In answer, she smiled and held the book aloft.

"I did," she said, "and left your friend wandering around in the trees, not knowing which direction was up."

Gabe frowned. "Did you hit him?"

Gwyn laughed. "I didn't have to," she said. "All I had to do was to turn him around a few times and he was so disorientated it will take him a month to find his way home." She handed him the book. "This is yours, I believe," she said. "I suggest we get back to the Abbey and let that nice Henry know where to find Ronan of Feldham. He won't get far on that ankle."

With that, she was gone, leaving Gabe to follow, with the Ateban Cipher clutched in his hand and a small smile on his face at hearing the man who was probably the King's fiercest soldier described as "that nice Henry."

Behind him, he could hear Damman calling out, his voice fading as he wandered farther into the trees. Ronan of Feldham was groaning in the dark, calling Damman a "silly fool," but his voice was not moving and for that Gabe was grateful.

As he climbed up onto Jasper, Gabe probed his conscience, looking for a sore spot, but discovered that he felt nothing but calm and relief. Gwyn was safe, the book was safe, and nobody had died.

Which made the day, despite everything, a good one.

❖

Was it really just a few months ago that he'd been in the hallway outside this office, hiding behind an urn? Looking around the Abbot's rooms, bright with candlelight and full of people, Gabe could hardly believe it was the same place.

The Abbot smiled at him, looking rested and happy behind his huge oak desk. The time he'd spent at Widow Goodman's farm had been good for the old man, Gabe thought, looking at the Abbot, who was fuller in the cheeks and less furrowed in the brow than Gabe could ever remember.

In the corner, Ralf Hodges sat in a deep armchair, his head bandaged with care by Brother Archibold, and his daughters snuggled beside him. While Gwyn and Gabe had been off rescuing the book, Henry and a party of soldiers had rescued the King's stag and the King had appointed Ralf his Royal Gamekeeper, granting him a lifetime's residency in the forest, and a small cottage for him and the girls, including Midge.

Midge was happy to have a family once again, though her joy was somewhat tempered by the fact that Albert had not been seen since his visit at the window at Rothwell Castle.

"I always knew he'd leave one day," she'd said quietly to Gabe when he'd asked about the falcon. "I'm glad he's chosen a happy day."

"But now," the Abbot said, breaking into Gabe's thoughts as he watched Midge flicking through the Ateban

Cipher. She'd asked Gabe for one last look at the beautiful pictures before the book was lost to her forever, and he'd been happy to oblige, knowing how much she loved it.

"We must talk about the book," he continued, looking at Gabe, who was still staring at Midge.

It was still a puzzle to Gabe that someone who loved books as much as she did struggled with her letters. He'd noticed that she could often read the first letter in a word, but then complain that the rest were just a jumbled mess. He made a resolution to ask the Abbot if she could continue her tuition somehow – and perhaps get to the root of the problem.

"Gabriel?" said the Abbot, and Gabe suddenly realized the entire room was looking at him.

"Sorry, Abbot," he said, blushing. "I was woolgathering."

"Indeed," the Abbot said, and Gabe was startled by the wink aimed at him. "As the keeper of the book, I wonder if you have given any thought as to what you will do next."

Startled, Gabe blinked. "I, er, well, I haven't had time to really consider . . ." he said, before breaking off, realizing that he didn't need to think about what happened next. "It can't stay here," he said. "Too many people know of its whereabouts."

It was the same argument that Lucien had given for not keeping it at Hayden's Mont, and it was true.

The Abbot nodded sadly. "I fear that this is true," he said. "The fact that it cannot be read will not stop those who want it. If it is not Lord Sherborne, it will be another, and they will never stop until they have unlocked its secrets."

"Um," said Midge, into the heavy silence that followed, but the Abbot held up one hand to silence her.

"So the decision you must make, young Gabriel, is whether you will appoint another as the keeper of the book and take your place here once again, safe, in your home."

Gabe swallowed, thinking about the familiar walls that surrounded him right now, and about how he knew every cobble, every blade of grass, every Brother inside those walls. Here, life was predictable. There were no decisions to make about right and wrong, no horrible moments of life and death, no heartbreak.

But even as these thoughts ran through his mind, Gabe found himself shaking his head.

The Abbot looked at him, surprised. "You do not wish this?" he asked.

Gabe walked over to kneel before the head of the Abbey. "I am the keeper of the book," he said. "It is up to me to keep it safe, to take it beyond these walls, to hide it from those who would expose its secrets."

"Er —" said Midge, and Gabe could hear her riffling the pages of the Ateban Cipher, though he did not look at her, keeping his eyes on the Abbot's wrinkled face.

The Abbot sighed. "I thought this would be your answer," he said. "So be it, young Gabriel. Be a light in the world, but come back to us should you ever need a safe haven."

Gabe bowed his head, feeling tears prick the backs of his eyes. "I will give you a mentor and companion," the Abbot continued. "You will not undertake this journey alone. Is there anyone in particular you would wish for?"

Gabe nodded. "Brother Malachy," he said, knowing without asking that the older Brother would relish the opportunity to revisit the world he'd fled so many years earlier.

"Very well, then," said the Abbot. "We are done here. I think it is time we all took to our beds. The sun will soon rise."

But Midge was now tugging on the back of Gabe's tunic. "Gabe," she said, as he turned to her. "Gabe, I can read this. I can read the book."

Gabe looked at her in astonishment as she opened the cover and turned to one of the first pages. He recognized the botanical illustration of the plant that looked like a snowdrop, its center a drop of gold.

"*Deep in the forests of Estadon, in the shade of the Golden Ash, lies the duplicitous Atternum flower, at once a bringer of death and the flora of eternal life,*" she read. "*Gathered in the daytime, it emits a somnolent scent, but picked in the full moon, on the first day of the eleventh month, it can be distilled into an eternal elixir.*"

"Stop!" roared the King as everyone else in the room gaped at Midge, who dropped the book in fright. "What sorcery is this?"

"It's okay," said Gabe, rushing to Midge's side, "it's not sorcery."

"What is it then?" gasped Scarlett. "Midge can't even read properly yet, Gabe, you know she can't. How can she possibly be reading a book that no one can read?"

"I think," said Gabe slowly, bending to pick up the book, "that Midge just sees letters and words differently from the way we do. And I think that whoever wrote this book perhaps saw them the same way."

The Abbot frowned. "Why would someone like that be chosen for such a task?" he asked.

"Because it allows the secrets of the book to be hidden in plain sight," said Gabe, the words tumbling out, almost unable to keep up with his thoughts. "Don't you see? Whoever wrote this would have known that only learned men would have access to it. Nobody has books unless they can *read* them, and it's only people like us, Abbot, or noblemen like the King and Scarlett's father, who can afford books, who can read. So the secrets of the book were forever safe."

The King nodded slowly. "I see," he said. "Nobody would ever give access to a valuable book to someone who'd never learned to read. And so the secrets remained hidden because somewhere, somehow, along the way, the additional secret of the key to the code wasn't passed down and so became lost."

"Exactly," said Gabe, putting an arm around Midge, his mind working furiously. "Until now. I think you not only need to be learning to read to decipher the code, but to be *struggling* to learn to read. Thereby adding an extra level of security."

The Abbot stood. "I am not certain whether to laugh or cry," he said, hands on his head. "For the code is cracked, making the book more dangerous than ever."

There was a short silence. "What if it's good?" said Gwyn, her eyebrows raised. "What if it's just full of things that could help people? Eternal life sounds pretty good."

Gabe knew she was thinking of her mother, which reminded him that he had left her precious teacup in the stables with Nicholas, who had decided to stay the night to tend to Delphine's sore leg.

It was the Abbot's turn to sigh. "If only that were true," he said. "But our world swings on a delicate balance. If we all lived forever, wouldn't our world soon be overrun? If we all turned lead to gold, wouldn't the value of gold turn to nothing? There is a difference between knowing you *can* do something and knowing that it's the right thing to do. Ancient lore suggests that the Ateban Cipher is full of such dilemmas." He paused, sitting back down in his chair. "Have you heard of Pandora's Box?" he asked.

When Gwyn shook her head, he continued. "It's an ancient story about a woman who went against all advice and opened a box she'd been given, releasing all of the evils into the world. It was a small act, but the consequences were larger than anyone could have ever imagined."

"And you think the Ateban Cipher is like that box?" asked Gwyn.

"I think that once its secrets are unlocked, we will not be able to put them back into the box, good or bad," said the Abbot. "For that reason, it is safer if no one knows where it is, or that the code has been cracked. We need time to think about what we should do next."

"Remind me again why we don't just throw it into the fire?" Merry chipped in.

"No!" This time it was Gabe, Midge, the Abbot and the King who raised their voices in protest.

"Just because a job is difficult does not mean we shirk it," the Abbot went on in his normal voice. "The Ateban Cipher has traveled far and wide, it has survived for centuries and its secrets have been kept safe."

"Plus," said Midge, dreamily, "it's beautiful."

"Indeed," said the King. "But the fact is that the secret of the key to the code must never leave this room and . . ." He paused, looking at Midge, a strange expression on his face. "I'm afraid, young lady, that means that you and the book must be kept apart. Knowing that you are the key, that you could read it to me, unlock its very secrets

for me . . . You cannot conceive of the power you hold."
The King turned to the Abbot. "Get it out of here," he
said, his face pained. "Now. This night. I do not trust
even myself."

The Abbot nodded, sadly. "You are a good man," he
said to the King, before turning to Gabe. "You must go,"
he said. "Take the book. Tell no one where you go. Do
not come back here unless you hear from me. I fear that
dark times are ahead of us and the book must be safe."

"But –" Gabe said, but the Abbot simply shook his
head, and Gabe's words stilled on his tongue. He wanted
to go to Hayden's Mont, to see Lucien, to discuss the book
and, he barely dared admit to himself, to see his mother.

"You must disappear," said the Abbot. "The book must
disappear."

Looking around at all the faces that had become so
dear to him, Gabe blinked back tears. He had left the
Abbey to save the book, desperate to come home. Now
he was to leave again.

He bowed to the King and to Eddie. "Your Majesty.
Your Highness," he said.

The King bowed back. "We owe you a great deal," he
said, putting an arm around Eddie. "And there is room
for you at the palace, as discussed."

"We will set aside a groom of the stool especially for
you," said Eddie, with a straight face.

The King's eyebrows almost hit his hairline as the girls erupted into giggles.

"We'll come and see you off," said Merry, pulling the other girls with her. "All of us."

Gabe tucked the book into the waistband of his breeches, as he followed them from the room towards the stables, deep in thought. He thought of the King's eyes as they'd assessed the book and Midge. He thought of the Abbot's talk of dark times, and of Lucien insisting that he take the book from Hayden's Mont.

"They know where it is," he'd said. *"They won't rest until they have it."*

And he knew what he had to do.

❖

"Goodbye, Abbot," Gabe said, kneeling to receive a blessing from the man who had been the head of his home for so long. "Thank you for everything."

"It is I who should thank you, young Gabriel," said the Abbot, putting one hand on Gabe's shoulder. "You will always have a home here."

"Move along, Sandals," said Gwyn, standing beside Jasper, who was saddled up and ready to go. "Adventure awaits. And we know how much you love that."

Rolling his eyes, Gabe walked towards Jasper and swung himself up into the saddle, feeling the swish of his robes tangling around his ankles as he did so. Malachy had suggested that Gabe travel in his novice's robes and sandals, making it easier to seek extended stays in far-off monasteries and abbeys, and Gabe had agreed, though he'd stuffed a set of breeches and a tunic in his saddlebags along with the worn boots he'd been wearing. Just in case.

"Ready?" asked Malachy, already atop his own mount, his gray hair bristling with excitement. As Gabe had thought, the older Brother had taken very little convincing to join him on his travels.

Gabe nodded, touching his heels to Jasper's side before suddenly halting the horse, as though he'd forgotten something.

"Wait!" he said, and Malachy also stopped. "I almost forgot. I have something for Gwyn."

With a small prayer, he handed the bundle to Gwyn, experiencing a small jolt of pleasure at having surprised her.

"Is this the King's pillowcase?" she said, her eyebrows drawn together. "Sandals, what have you been up to?"

"It's your teacup," Gabe said with a grin and a wave as he urged Jasper forward. "Open it later. By yourself."

She frowned, and Gabe knew that she'd felt the weight of the bundle, but she nodded. He followed Malachy from the stables, towards the gates he'd last ridden through under very different circumstances.

Gabe knew that Gwyn would open the bundle and gasp. For nestled in beside the precious teacup was the Ateban Cipher, and his hastily scrawled note.

Dear Gwyn, as the keeper of the book it's up to me to keep it safe. As I ride to Hayden's Mont, I can think of no safer place for it to be than with you. Don't tell the others. If they don't know, they can't tell. Just hide it as only you can, away from Midge, and I'll be back for it as soon as I can. Gabe.

❖

Gabe breathed out, watching the cloud of steam drift off into the night air.

Nudging Jasper forward, Gabe turned to look back over his shoulder, down the hill to where Oldham Abbey stood – dark, silent, solid. The bells for matins would ring soon enough, but for now, the Abbey slept.

"Which way?" Malachy asked, and Gabe realized they'd reached the crossroads on the Rothwell Road.

"North," said Gabe, firmly turning Jasper in that direction, hearing Malachy do the same. "We'll go to Hayden's Mont. We'll tell Lucien what has happened."

We'll see my mother, he added silently. It wouldn't be easy, he knew, untangling his feelings and the story of his origins, but it was something he needed to do.

"It's good to be on the road again," said Malachy, sounding content despite the lateness of the hour and the chill in the air.

"It is," said Gabe, suddenly realizing that he meant the words. "It is."

Off in the woods, deep in the impenetrable darkness, Gabe heard a five-note whistle and smiled, before pursing his lips and answering with the same tune. Was she watching, he wondered? Shadowing them as they rode? Or did Gwyn somehow just know, with that uncanny instinct of hers, just where he would be right now?

Gabe felt a strange sense of peace come over him, even as he rode away from everything he'd known. The Abbey would still be there when he was ready to return. And Gwyn's signal suggested that she had read his note. She and his other friends would be waiting when he returned for the book.

And in the meantime, Gwyn would put it where she wanted, when she wanted, and no one would ever find it unless she wanted them to.

ACKNOWLEDGEMENTS

I have enjoyed beyond belief the opportunity to unlock the secrets of new worlds and characters with Gabe, Merry, Gwyn, Scarlett, Midge and Eddie, but it's so much easier to do so when you have a stable team around you.

Thank you to Jo Butler and the team at Cameron's for guiding the journey, and to the intrepid team at Hachette Australia, particularly Suzanne O'Sullivan, Kate Stevens, Tom Bailey-Smith, Chris Kunz, Ashleigh Barton, Fiona Hazard, Justin Ractliffe and Louise Sherwin-Stark, as well as cover designers Blacksheep and illustrator Paul Young.

Thank you to my extended family with love and to my friends (you know who you are) who continue to keep my feet on the ground while my head remains firmly in the clouds.

A special thank you to my first readers Sophie, Jody, Anna, Georgia, Lilly, Joe and Lucas, who took Gabe and his friends to heart from the opening lines and encouraged me all the way.

And, as always, all my love to my boys: John, Joseph and Lucas. Every book is for you.

A. L. TAIT

Adventure and danger lie just
off the edge of the map…

A. L. Tait grew up dreaming of world domination. Unfortunately, at the time there were only alphabet sisters B. L. and C. A. and long-suffering brother M. D. M. to practice on . . . and parents who didn't look kindly upon sword fights, plank walking or bows and arrows. But dreams don't die and The Mapmaker Chronicles and The Ateban Cipher, the author's two series for children, are the result. A. L. lives in country New South Wales, Australia, with a family, a garden, three goldfish and a very cheeky border collie. A. L. Tait writes fiction and nonfiction for adults under another name.